Ma Mae's Legacy

Ma Mae's Legacy

Short Stories

Melva Archer-Persico

Ma Mae's Legacy

ISBN: 978-0-9908498-2-7
Library of Congress Control Number: 2019911867

TABLE OF CONTENTS

"It takes more than one life to make a person." - Pauline Melville – *The Ventriloquist's Tale*

The wonderful women of the Johnson-Archer and Ferrier clans have been my inspiration. Many have passed away - I salute the wonderful memories that remain of them. To those who are still with us - I salute you too and dedicate this book to you.

MA MAE'S HOUSE

The sound of sawing and hammering filled the air. A small pile of termite-eaten wood lay in a corner near the front fence. Soon it would all be burned, along with the nest the workers had found. The carpenters were busy sawing and nailing the new boards in place. It was mainly the window frames and sills that had succumbed to the destructive gnawing of those annoying termites. In a matter of hours with a fresh coat of white paint, the house looked like new again.

High and proud, on its concrete pillars, the house stood out on the narrow pot-holed street. Bright, white paint graced its walls, and its awning and casement windows always welcomed the abundant smells and sounds that wafted in on balmy breezes. This was Ma Mae's house: a house built bit by bit on land bought with years of accumulated box hands and the proceeds from her sale of ground cocoa, guava jelly, guava cheese and other sweetmeats. There was very little idle time for those who dwelled here. A 'work-house' is what some called it when they were out of Ma Mae's earshot, of course. She, however, knew that hard work brought fine results. This was one of the many lessons she passed on to those in her charge.

Maybeline Lewis stood tall and stately. Well into her eighties, she carried herself with a regality that harkened back to the

Ancient Continent of her fore-parents. Born at the turn of the century, she was the proud grandchild of John Thomas, who together with his wife Caroline, were among the last batch of enslaved Africans to be shipped to British Guiana from West Africa before the slave trade ended. She was barely out of her teens when love and marriage to Festus Lewis took her on a sixty-year journey of "for better and for worse" and "till death do us part." She really believed in those promises and did her best to keep them faithfully. Motherhood was a badge she wore with honour, and it was with great fondness that the children she bore and the many she nurtured alongside these, all called her Ma Mae. She it was, who ruled the roost in that white, wooden house where manners, respect, and proper etiquette reigned.

"Manners maketh man!" was a mantra she drilled into her charges. "With good manners and a solid education, you will go far in this world. In my day, sixth standard was the most schooling we could get. Now y'all have the opportunity to go to high school and even higher. Make the most of it! Don't take your schooling for granted."

CLICK-CLACK-CLICK-CLACK

She stretched her neck, leaned back her head against the wooden rocker, and sighed deeply. Nobody could say she hadn't done her best. A faint smile filled with quiet pride played lightly on the corners of her mouth as she reflected on how well they had all done: Claire, a teacher, Joseph, an

electrician, Baldwin, an education officer, Sandra, a nurse...
The sound of a car horn tooting disturbed her reveries. She
leaned forward and looked through the window. Philip was
passing on his way up the East Bank to take care of his civil
service duties. She waved to him as he drove off. She shook
her head and smiled, this time with incredulity.

<< *I would have never believed it if someone had told me Philip
would have become a big Government official! That boy didn't like
school! He was always up to some trick or the other to get away
from going to school. Now look at him, driving fancy cars and
making all kind of speeches on the radio!*>>

A quiet laugh escaped her lips as she recalled her great-
nephew's escapades. She would never forget the day Janie
had called her with the news. "Ma Mae, Phillip in hospital. I
don't know wha' wrong with him. Since he wake this
morning, he ain't talking and the doctors can't tell me is wha'
wrong with him." When Ma Mae went to the hospital that
afternoon, she tried to engage the patient in conversation.
"Phillip boy, Ma Mae come to see you. How you feeling?"
Silence.
"You can't talk?"
He shook his head.

Ma Mae proceeded to examine the patient – forehead, eyes,
mouth, ears, back… As she examined, she did the usual
massaging of the limbs, back and chest with liniment. She
then turned to her niece and said, "Well girl, he certainly

won't be able to write his exam if he's so sick." As she was leaving, Ma Mae kissed the patient tenderly on his forehead and said consolingly, "Phillip, Ma Mae going now. You want me to bring ice cream when I coming tomorrow?"

"Yes thanks, Ma Mae!" Phillip responded eagerly.

"Well, well, what a miraculous recovery!" Ma Mae declared. Turning to her niece she said, "Look Janie, carry this child home! Nothing ain't wrong with him! The lil scamp making a fool of you. No wonder the doctors can't find what's wrong with him!"

<<*That Phillip! In time he had settled down. And look at him now!*>>

She unwound her gnarled fingers and examined them. Her hands bore the sheen that could only have come from countless years of washing clothes soaked in bleach and harsh soap powder. As she lowered them to smooth the pleats on the front of her faded cotton house-dress, she thought about how quiet her house was now without the young ones around. She got up and walked over to the radio, turned it on and practically jumped back as the speakers assaulted her with "RAGA-RAGA-RAGA-RAGA!" She immediately switched off the radio but then turned it on again, but this time with the volume down low. "Is all kinda noise and shouting they playing on the radio these days," she grumbled as she eased herself back in to the rocker. "I need the company of the radio, though. I don't have the children and grandchildren to keep me busy. They really kept me on my toes," she chuckled.

<<*That Tommy, despite knowing what I stood for he was always trying to see how far he could go...* >>

He had shuffled up to her, invitation in hand, "Ma Mae... my friend invite me to his birthday party... on Saturday." Ma Mae accepted the invitation and put it in her apron pocket. Saturday afternoon came and Tommy, dressed in his party clothes, came to say goodbye. "Going Ma Mae," he announced.
"Going where?" she inquired.
"To the party, Ma Mae. You remember I showed you the invitation?"
"Spell Michael, boy."
Tommy sounded out each letter boldly, "M – I – C – H – E – A – L!"
As soon as he finished, Mae Mae retrieved the invitation from her pocket and replied, "Oh, yes? Now you go and take off your clothes, and when Michael learns to spell *his* name, *then* you can go to the party!"

<<*Could you believe it! He must be thought I born yesterday! From the time I laid eyes at that invitation, I knew he had made it himself. They're right when they say 'God knows why grandparents don't make children.' But things different now-a-days. Both parents have to go out to work and somebody has to help*

them out with the children. Oh, those grandchildren! If it wasn't one thing, it was another. That Maggie! She think I didn't know she was sending a note to the Wilson boy? Now tell me what she wanted with boyfriend at twelve! She was too force-ripe! I had to put a quick stop to that.>>

Dear Arnold and Anne,

Greetings in the name of our Lord and Saviour. I hope this letter finds you and the children well. We at this end are all in good health, thank God.

I am sending you this note I found. Maggie wrote it to the Wilson boy in the next street. As you know, I am a strict mother and grandmother. So I don't encourage slackness. Maggie is too young to be thinking about boys. At her age, she should be concentrating on her lessons. I think that you as parents should deal with the situation before it gets out of hand.

I close now with all my love to both of you, and hugs and kisses for the children.

Your loving mother,

Ma Mae.

<<I'm sure Maggie must be happy that we didn't encourage her with her nonsense! She got over that boyfriend phase, studied her lessons and now she is a Bank Manager with a nice family. As for the Wilson boy, what a waste! He still playing a sweet-boy around the town with about five different children-mothers!>>

The insistent chimes of the wall clock roused her from her musings. It was four o'clock, time for afternoon tea. She leaned over, placed her feet securely in her once-blue, flour-spattered bedroom slippers, eased herself out of the chair and made her way slowly to the kitchen, stopping on the way to turn up the volume on the radio. "Parts arrive for the Power Plant. Blackouts will soon be a thing of the past." "Boat capsizes in the Pomeroon, six dead." "President leaves for state visit to Thailand." "We'll be back with the news after a word from our sponsors."

The only bright spot in the news was the prospect of an end to blackout. She munched on her salt biscuits and guava jelly and sipped her cup of milky, green tea. The shouts and laughter of the children making their way home from school punctuated her solitude.

<<*Those grandchildren really kept us busy. That Gwen! She always wanted to be the first one to get to the table. She would try to get away with not washing her hands. And Calvin, that boy had a long stomach. He was never satisfied. Pa would always remind him, "Boy this is only a snack to keep the worms in check. Be content with what your grandmother gave you!"*>>

The children's voices fading further and further in the distance, the drone of the radio announcer's voice, the constant whirring and intermittent bang from the old fridge, the perennial tick-tock of the wall clock and the occasional creak of windows as their hinges resisted the constant breezes, accompanied her reflections. The morning hours were her busy time - cooking, cleaning, laundry... There was little time to think then. She usually spent the long afternoon hours listening to the radio, reading, crocheting or just looking back on life...

Back in her favourite spot, she rocked back and forth. Once-vibrant eyes, now dimmed and slightly yellowed, were half-closed in reflection. A head of silver reclined on carved wood and long, sturdy fingers tapped out a slow rhythm on the chair-arm to accompany the song on the radio.

In the same way that she had kept her children and grandchildren in line, Ma Mae always ensured that her surroundings were spic and span. The house received a fresh coat of paint every year. She left nothing to chance. Wood-ants and humidity were close friends, but Ma Mae saw to it that they did not destroy her prized possession.

CLICK-CLACK-CLICK-CLACK
CLICK-CLACK-CLICK-CLACK

Yes, life had been good but there were some times she would much rather forget. She looked at the wooden window frames, got up and went over to examine them closely. "Who would have believed," she mused "with all the care I took, the wood-ants still tried to take over." They had started to burrow into the wooden casings and nibble away at them until they became paper-thin. The window frames were the first victims of their assault. Her quick, decisive action and constant vigilance had saved her windows and her entire house. She ran her fingers along the smooth, wooden frames and went back to her rocker.

CLICK-CLACK-CLICK-CLACK

Claire would be home soon, and she would have some company for the rest of the evening.

"No New Year's Day... I just called..."
Now that's music," she thought tapping her feet and bobbing her head to the beat.
"... I mean it from the bottom..." The telephone's ring cut into the melody. Claire had called to say she had a late meeting and wouldn't be home in time for dinner. Ma Mae made her way downstairs to lock up the fowls and to make sure everything was secure. Climbing the stairs was especially hard for her today. She held on to the rails with both hands and pulled herself up one foot at a time. By the time she dropped herself into the Berbice chair, cold sweat covered her entire body. She pulled the crumpled handkerchief from the pocket of her dress, mopped her brow, closed her eyes and breathed in and out deeply, all the while praying silently. The feeling soon passed. "I have to tell Dr. Ashook about these feelings the next time I go to see him" she thought. "They've been happening every few days."

She reached into the basket on the floor next to the chair and picked up the crochet thread and needle. She decided to finish the chair backs she was making for Godfrey's wife while waiting for Claire to get home. As she settled down to work, the neighbours' voices drifted in through the open window with the cool evening breeze.

"Gyurl Shirley, you hear the news?"
"Wha' news?
"Doris small daughter gettin' baby!"

<<*Oh, how they love a juicy talk-name in this town! If it wasn't Doris daughter or Boysie son, it was someone else. I could imagine how they must have been running their mouths about me all those years ago...* >>

"Y'all hear? Mrs. Lewis like she goin' out she head!"
"Who tell you so? The family say is she thyroid gat she sick like duh!"
"Thyroid my foot! Is the shame and scandal!"
"Hmm! No wonder! What she husband do would send anybody out dey head!"
"Lord, what a thing, eh! He does look so pious and always in the church! I hear is a lil girl from up de coast!"

<<*They must have gone on and on, making her business their own. And maybe they had a right to talk. It was scandalous indeed. I knew the child. She was a child, and a family-friend at that! They say 'when yuh gat yuh dutty calico don't hang it outside!" But this*

one could not be hidden. Lord, you gave me the strength! It wasn't always easy but how could I, as a Christian woman, blame a child for the failings of his father? The lil god-angel ain't do me a thing! All I could do was love Godfrey like my own. That stilled their wagging tongues too!>>

Ma Mae held up the chair back to the light and admired the pattern. It was well-done. It carried the image of a house and the words "Home is where the heart is." She was pleased with her handiwork. She folded it and put it with the others in the basket. She hoped Godfrey and Lynette would be happy with it. It was seven o'clock.

"Parts arrive for the Power Plant. Blackouts will soon be a thing of the past." "Boat capsizes in the Pomeroon, six dead." "President leaves for state visit to Thailand." She switched off the radio. It was the same old news. A feeling of extreme tiredness accompanied by an urgent need to relieve herself overcame her. She didn't think she could wait up for Claire.

Claire closed the gate and secured it with the padlock. The rattling of keys as she fumbled to open the door cut through the thick rustic silence. Not even the dogs were barking tonight. The silence entered with her and seemed to precede her up the stairs and into the living room. Something just wasn't right.

Ma Mae was not in her usual place in the rocking chair near the window. She was not in the Berbice chair near the radio.

Maybe she decided to turn in early. But why hadn't she turned off the lights? The feeling of uneasiness she had felt as she entered the house increased almost to the point of panic.

"Ma Mae! Ma Mae!" she called as she made her way hurriedly toward the bedroom.

The hearse drove slowly up the street toward Ma Mae's house. Alma ran into the street and threw herself on the hood of the vehicle. Her ear-piercing wail shattered the silence of the humid afternoon. "Why? Why? Why? Ow Charlie, not even a goodbye? Wha' gon' happen to dem lil children?"she wailed and banged her fists into the car even as her sisters Jane and Claire tried to console her.

Claire glanced over at her eldest sister, Alma. She was very composed, there were no signs of the excessive grief she had displayed thirty years before when her brother had died suddenly in a car accident. She mopped her brow with the edge of her apron and continued serving lunch to those who had made the long trip to Berbice. They were all here again. Everyone had come from far and wide to say their farewells to Ma Mae.

The gilded casket looked out-of-place on the brick-like mud below the wooden house on concrete pillars. Sky-blue taffeta, ivory satin and the ashen look of too much white talcum powder on mahogany skin combined with the lilting sound of Jim Reeves' hymns.

CLICK-CLACK-CLICK-CLACK...

Everyone turned and looked, and then they all stood to greet Ma Mae's offspring as they descended the stairs: beautiful shoots of a fallen mangrove. They stood as firmly as the sturdy concrete pillars that held up the house Ma Mae had built. They smiled, hugged, shook hands and celebrated their mother's ninety-odd years of life, determined to hold true to the remarkable legacy she had left for them and for generations to come.

MIGNON'S PRIZE

The wedding portrait graced her bedside table. Out of habit, she picked it up and relived that wonderful day fifteen years ago. She wasn't dressed in bridal attire, but it was her wedding day. A simple string of faux pearls, a little button hat and her bouquet of fresh yellow daffodils and chrysanthemums accessorized her chic, cream crepe skirt suit and matching shoes. He was as dapper as ever in his dark, pinstriped suit. A single yellow rose was pinned unto the lapel. His wavy hair was slick and parted stylishly down the center of his head. The smile on her face revealed her pride and happiness.

She had looked forward to that day for so many years! Which girl didn't? She was no different from her friends. That was their goal: marriage, a ring, the title of 'Mrs' before her name. She finally had her prize! It was high time! She was approaching thirty! Some people had even started whispering about her being an old-maid who had been left on the shelf and the tune she heard every time she travelled to the city to visit her mother had become like a scratched record: "Girl, when you gon' give me a son-in-law, eh? Wait, they don't have any eligible bachelors up-the-river?"

She worked as a teacher at one of the best schools in the mining town and her parents, especially her father, loved to boast about her. "Bertie, you see my daughter, Mignon?

She's a teacher, you know? Bright girl!" Her father was proud to introduce her to his friends. The irony of it all never failed to bring a smile to her face. Her father hadn't even wanted her to attend high school. "I don't have money to waste on no gyurl chile. She could stay home and learn to sew and cook. Just now she goin' to find a husband and get married." Thanks to her mother's insistence, she had attended high school and later qualified herself as a trained teacher.

Training College was a lot of hard work, but it was fun too. How she enjoyed the end-of- term dances! She revelled in all the latest moves like the twist and ska. Oh, and when it came time to waltz, sailing across the floor in Mike's arms felt like heaven. Mike! Her career almost ended because of him. *Yes, Mike lived up to their favourite tune. He really was a playboy. The dancing at the parties often led to lovers' lane at the seawall... I would never forget my mother's distress when I told her ...*

"Gyurl is wha' kinna crosses you bringin' on we now?" She held her head in her hands as she plopped down into the sofa. " Now when you jus' graduate from college, you tellin' me wha? You gon have to go up to Essequibo by Cousin Annie 'til next year! Lord! Your father must be de known why he didn't want you to go to no college."

She gave birth to her son, Jason, on the tenth of June, 1955 in Essequibo, far away from the curious eyes and wagging tongues of those who knew her. It was a great relief when she got the teaching job up-river. Nobody there knew her business. She still longed for a husband, though. *My son needs a father. I can't continue to have him living in my mother's home, and hear her responding to people's questions about him with her usual lie: "He's an adoption."*

In the dusty, mining town she now called home, she made many new friends and of course, that's where she met him. Tall, dark, handsome, charismatic, didn't only come from fictional works. There he was in real-life, in the flesh, before her eyes.

"Good afternoon Miss. I understand you have a problem with the fuses in this classroom?"

"Oh, oh yes. The fuse box is in the corner over there."

Goodness gracious! The Headmistress had told her an electrician was coming to fix the fuses during the lunch break, but she didn't expect a mahogany prince! "All done, Miss. Are you new on the staff? I've never seen you before. I'm Jerry Floris." They chatted for a while, and then, "You really need to get out and meet some more people in the area. My church is having an ice-cream banquet next Saturday, why not come with me. I have an extra ticket." *My, my! He was quite a catch! Could a girl ask for more, a handsome, skilled tradesman and a church-going one at that?!*

Mignon found it hard to give her full attention to her teaching that afternoon. The closely cropped hair, almond eyes and full lips in a face of dark, rich mahogany kept invading her consciousness…

…………...............

The skirt suit fit perfectly and did a good job of hiding her thickening waistline… Ms. Ines was a skilled seamstress.

"Oh no! This couldn't be happening again! Paula, I missed my period!" She often reflected on her friend's reassuring words, "Don't worry. I'm sure Jerry will do the right thing. Don't panic. Look, wasn't it just a few weeks ago that he took you to meet his family?"

Yes, he had taken her to Bartica to meet his family. That had to mean something, right? Her prayers were answered! Jerry didn't let her down. He did what was right. It didn't matter that his family refused to come. She had her prize! Her baby would have a father.

The button hat that topped off her wedding outfit was the rage of the fifties. Some people even added feathers, flowers or veils to them. Hers was simple, free of adornment. It sat snugly on her pageboy haircut.

There was no time or money to plan a big wedding. It was just as well, neither of their parents would be there: his because they disapproved of his leaving the village girl high and dry and hers, because of a different kind of disapproval.

"You couldn't find somebody closer to your own colour? The two of y'all like black and white whiskey!" She couldn't believe her ears! She knew her father could not possibly think they were white! Sure, they were not as dark as Jerry, but in this country of six races and all kinds of mixtures, no one should be pig-headed in matters of race. He had prevented her mother from coming to the wedding. Their absence hurt her, but she didn't allow that to cast a cloud over her special day. She was happy. She now had a handsome, caring, intelligent god-fearing man.

His right hand was around her waist, exactly as the photographer had directed him. The left hand rested lightly on the satin-gloved hands that held a bouquet of daffodils and chrysanthemums...

Her slim, delicate fingers slowly stroked the cool glass that protected their wedding portrait. They then clenched into a fist as she remembered the first time Jerry's dark side reared its head. His best friend Ralph and his wife, Dora had come to visit. Mignon saw this as the perfect opportunity to tell Ralph about her plan to surprise Jerry.

"You know, Ralph, I'd like to plan a surprise party for Jerry to celebrate his promotion. Can you help me with some of the arrangements? You know I'll need to get drinks and so..." Ralph was only too willing to assist.
"Sure Mignon. I'll come on Friday afternoon for us to... I

tell you Mignon times have really changed." Ralph had changed the subject quickly when he saw Jerry entering the room. Mignon remember that Jerry's jaw had tightened as he aked, "Is what the two o' y'all whispering about?"

Their visitors had barely left before the interrogation began: "Is what you and Ralph been talking about?"
"Oh, nothing important," she smiled and patted him on the cheek. Jerry pushed her hand away roughly, snapping as he did so, "So you making plans with man behind my back!" Mignon was surprised at Jerry's insinuations, but she was determined not to make a scene. "Come on Jerry, Honey. There's no need to be worried. You don't trust me? There's no need to be insecu..." Before she could finish her sentence Jerry snarled, "Don't think you can bamboozle me with you sweet talk! I ain't no teacher but I'm not a fool either." With that he shoved her into the house and slammed the door shut. As she turned to face him, surprised at the outburst, her face was whipped in the opposite direction as he dealt her a forceful back-hand slap. She fell to the floor sobbing. His fingers had stung her face, but she felt even more pain in her heart. *Why? Why?*
She held her head between her hands and sobbed quietly. She could hear Jerry on the phone…
"Hello, Dora? Let me have a word with Ralph. Ralph, look, is me, Jerry. Is wha' you and Mignon really up to?
Y'all feel … Oh, oh, okay. Oh, I now understand why y'all didn't tell me? You're a real friend man. Thanks."

Jerry was on his knees, begging forgiveness as he held an ice pack to her face. "I'm sorry Sweetie. I just thought Ralph was hustling you and I saw red. I promise it won't happen again. I love you baby." He cradled her in his arms and carried her to bed. The following day he bought her roses and they celebrated with a special dinner of her favourite dish that he insisted on preparing.

Jerry's promotion party was no longer a surprise, but it turned out to be an enjoyable event. Their friends came and they danced the night away.

True to his word, Jerry never hit her again. After the birth of their daughter Marissa, Jason, her first born, came to live with them. Jerry was proud of both children and treated Jason as his own. Mignon was ecstatic! Life could not have been better...

She had bought the cream patent leather pumps at Bettencourts. They were about a half size too small, but she had fallen in love with them and as they were the same colour as her outfit, she decided to take them. It was her special day. She had to look her best...

To the people in their town, she and Jerry were a fashionable couple. They always wore the latest styles and looked their best when they went out to various functions.
It was fun going down to Main street where all the best shops were, sometimes with Jerry and at other times with her

friend Paula, to shop or just window shop. How she missed those days...

The whirring of the ceiling fan accompanied Mignon's thoughts as she lay in bed trying to rest before beginning her evening chores and preparations for another week ahead. As she tossed and turned the whirring overhead soon became the buzz of Jerry's constant accusations and insinuations ringing in her head:
"Mignon, is where you went to this midday? I passed by the school and you weren't there? You like to walk about nuh?" "Listen Mignon, I don't like you just going out like that without telling me." "So why you must take these children to Georgetown to spend the August holidays? Why y'all can't stay right here?" "Woman, I didn't tell you that this Friday night bingo affair is trouble? Those women you going out with ain't married. They gon lead you astray." "But is why your friend Paula always calling, calling? She want you to end up in the divorce court like she, nuh?" "No, we're not going to the staff social. Your teacher friends feel they better than people like me."

Mignon tried her best to make Jerry happy. Despite his insecurities he was loving and kind. He now did all the marketing, took them to church, concerts and outings and he was a good father to the children. Maybe he was right. She should spend more time taking care of the children instead of gallivanting about the place with her unmarried workmates.

The bouquet of yellow daffodils and chrysanthemums that complemented her outfit was unconventional, but it matched the single yellow rose in Jerry's lapel. The portrait took her back to happier times - to a time of hope. What was it that her literature teacher had said about yellow roses and chrysanthemums? She couldn't remember. All she could think about on her wedding day was her prize! Her Jerry...

Jerry was a really good provider. He was so busy working they hardly saw him. At first, she would wait up for him. On the nights when he didn't come, she cried herself to sleep. She tried to be extra loving and kind when he did show up. Always the optimist, she just knew that her happiness resided with Jerry and soon things would be as good, or even better than when they first got married. What with her work, his work, the children and now another one on the way... maybe after this one things would return to normal...

It was Sunday evening. Jerry had been home all weekend. They were sitting listening to the programme of classical music on the radio after having put the children to bed.

His arm was around her shoulder and as he stroked her hair, he said, "You know Mignon. I don't think you should go back to work after the baby. I can provide adequately for all of us. You just concentrate on taking care of the house and the children." That bombshell had exploded without warning. She liked her job. She liked the freedom of being away from the home for a few hours every day. She liked the interaction with the children and other staff members. She didn't want to give it up. Mignon felt something dry-up in her that night. She knew deep down inside that what Jerry was doing wasn't right but what could she do? Where could she go?

She could no longer go out to work but she could use her teaching skills to help her children do well at school. She devoted her energies to taking care of the home and the children. They were all doing very well. Her eldest son was now at university and the other two were in high school. She no longer cried herself to sleep at nights. When she was finished helping the children with their homework, she got busy with her own studies. Her friend Paula was now living abroad, and she had signed her up for a correspondence course. She would soon complete the final module and then she'd receive her Diploma.

The wedding band was visible on the ring finger of the hand holding the bouquet.

She replaced the wedding photograph on the bedside table, removed the wedding ring and placed it next to the photograph. She did this quite often now. She walked over to the window and looked out on the heavy, gray clouds that were forming in the eastern sky. Rain was imminent. She had been Mrs. Floris for the past fifteen years. But where was Mr. Floris? Jerry only visited home occasionally now. Oh, he had kept his word, all right! They were never hungry. They were always well-clad and they lived in a comfortable home. She turned away from the window just as the first clap of thunder shattered the mid-afternoon peace. At precisely the same moment the phone started ringing.

"Hello?"

"Mrs.Floris?"

"Yes, this is she."

"Well madam, you can sit up there in yuh fancy house and play the lady! "She strained to decipher the words. The crackling static on the line and the thunder in the background made it difficult. The female voice was just confirming what she knew all along though. "But the nerve of that tramp! To call my house!" She didn't even try to control the rage that caused her to tremble as she replaced the receiver and made her way out on to the porch. She was oblivious to the cool sprays that blew in on her as she rocked back and forth. Her emotions fluctuated between outrage and gratitude for the call. Maybe she didn't need to know... Maybe she could have gone on with life the way it had been for the past several years... But knowledge is power. Now she knew for sure; she could do something about it.

That Saturday, in the wee hours of the morning, her brother arrived. She had spent all week preparing, so it didn't take them long to load everything on to the truck.

"Come on Mignon, let's go," her brother shouted. "The children are already in the truck."

"Okay, give me a minute. There's one more thing I have to take care of," she replied.

She entered the house, clutching the wedding portrait close to her chest. Her footsteps echoed on the wooden floor as she strode toward the bedroom. The house was now empty, except for the matrimonial bed. Jerry could do whatever he wanted to with *that*, she reasoned. On entering the room, she smashed the portrait against the wooden headboard and exhaled as what seemed like a thousand pieces of glass scattered every which way on the floor and the bed. She didn't care to see what her actions had done to the faces of the young couple. As she turned to leave the room, she ripped the ring off finger and threw it in the direction of the smashed portrait. With head held high, shoulders thrown back and a bounce in her stride, Mignon slammed the door shut and left.

She dozed for most of the two-hour drive to the city and woke to the scent of recent rain on hot asphalt. The sun had risen, and its golden rays were forcing their way through a smattering of gray clouds. She hugged her children close to her and smiled as she saw the hint of a rainbow on the horizon.

AND SO, SHE WROTE

Chantal could not believe her eyes; after so many years of wondering and sometimes looking, she had finally found it. There it was, tucked away at the bottom of the suitcase. This same old, brown suitcase had moved with her from her parents' home to her own home when she got married. She had not opened it in ages. Now, as she was preparing for her big move overseas, and trying to decide on what she really wanted to keep and what she had to get rid of, there it was - her treasured keepsake box. She reached in and lifted it out carefully. It seemed a bit heavier than she remembered. She tried unsuccessfully to keep from sneezing as she dusted off the thin film of dust that had gathered on the sturdy cardboard box. In it were her report cards from thirty-odd years ago and old autograph books from high school days. Gingerly, she lifted out the papers and hand-made autograph books, but there was something else in the box. She couldn't believe her eyes. The faded pink flowers still gave a cheery look to the olive-green leather cover of a book that held so many of her fondest memories.

"This is how it all began," she thought, as she traced out the once-gold embossed initials C.S that adorned the lower right corner of the cover. She sat on the floor, her back against the wall and started flipping through the yellowing pages...

July 21, 1972

Today Mom and I travelled to Berbice. I always enjoy riding in the train and then getting on the steamer...

The sound, the smells, they all came back to her as she read...

"Fish an' bre-ead! Fi-ish an' bre-ead!" The shrill voices of the vendors penetrated the train carriages as they walked up and down the platform attempting to catch the attention of hungry travellers.

"Mommy, I'm hungry, please buy one for me!" I longed to savour the taste of what appeared to be an especially delicious treat – well-seasoned fried fish in a six inch elongated roll of white bread with hot pepper sauce as a relish. My mother though, would have none of it: "Girl, stop being bad-fashion! You know how those people make that ting? Is not good to eat about! Look, I have some cheese and bread here. Eat this!"

Choo! Choo! The train's whistle announced its impending departure. I slumped back into my seat and chomped sullenly on the cheese sandwich my mother had thrust into my hand. Soon we were off again, leaving the pungent smell of the vendors' fried fish behind.

I always looked forward to the train rides from Georgetown to Rosignol and back. There was something special about watching the coconut plantations, rice farms, grazing livestock and old cottages that sped by as the train made its way from the city through numerous small villages. Mahaicony... Eldorado... Belladrum... Litchfield... We chugged past village after village of women at washtubs, boys tending sheep, donkey carts laden with drums of water and children playing cricket. I couldn't tell if the boys who stopped their games to wave, saw me waving back frantically at them. The smell of fresh cow dung, herbs, spices and fresh, ripe fruit wafted into the cabin. I closed my eyes and inhaled deeply. I was in Berbice! I loved going to my grandparents' home. I couldn't wait to show off my present to my cousins and to my good friend Darlene. I wished the train would go faster. Hopetown ... 29 ... 28. Mom and I tried to see who would guess the names of the villages correctly... Fort Wellington... Rosignol.

At Rosignol, we made our way up the wooden ramp into the ferry with extra special care. I made sure not to look down. Way down below, the muddy waters of the Berbice River swished and slapped against the boat. Once I had dared to look down and had almost missed my step. Had Mom not been there to grab hold of me... No. I preferred not to think of it. We headed out to the deck to enjoy the strong, fresh breezes, the lapping of the waves and the anticipation of the approaching eastern shore. This was definitely better than sitting inside where the acrid odour of filthy toilets assaulted our nostrils.

Mr. Lucas' taxi was at the stelling as usual, ready to take us on the last leg of our journey. I grabbed on to the back of the seat in front of me as the car swerved from side to side and bounced in and out of potholes. From my vantage point in the back seat, I listened as my mother answered his questions and enquired about his family. You would think she knew them the way she asked about them. I found myself trying to envision Mr. Lucas with his wife and five children - a short, stocky, very dark man with receding hairline and small, beady eyes that peered out from behind thick, horn-rimmed glasses. His wife would be a slightly shorter, fat, demure-looking brown woman dressed in a pleated, cotton dress, her jet-black hair pressed straight and hanging in limp, greasy strings around her face. Their five children, ranging in ages from ten to two, would look like stair treaders. They would all have small beady eyes and look like miniature versions of Mr. and Mrs. Lucas. The bumpity, bumpity, bump of the gravel road brought me to the edge of my seat. I leaned out the window to get my first glimpse of my grandparents' home.

I bounded up the stairs, trying my best to get through all the rituals as quickly as possible -   the hugging, wet kisses, questions about my behavior and performance in school... I could hardly wait to begin having fun with my cousins. Before I could put on my house clothes properly though, Aunty Mildred was hovering over me like a hawk. "Pick up those clothes and put them on a hanger! Put your shoes under the bed! You don't have no maid here to pick up after you!" I drew a long, silent schuups, glancing around to make sure no sound had escaped my lips.

My hunger and the tasty meal were no match for the excitement of seeing my cousins again. We ignored the admonitions of the grown-ups and chatted non-stop during lunch, trying to catch up on all that had taken place during our eleven months apart.

"Dis afternoon, leh we play dolly house! I gon' show y'all my new talkin' dolly."
"Wait till y'all see my diary!" I chimed in excitedly, "I gon show y'all when we finish eatin'."
"A diary? Wha' kin' o' present is duh?" They all laughed at my present. I was hurt. I had walked with my diary to keep track of my adventures this year. I guess I would just have to wait until I returned home to do that. I tried to redeem myself with my cousins by telling them about all the features of my toy fridge. "It has eggs, cabbage, chicken and real ice trays," I boasted.

"Children! Stop the talking and eat your lunch! You shouldn't talk and eat at the same time, you will choke! And take your elbows of the table!" Aunt Mildred was her usual strict, serious self. We couldn't relax with her around. She seemed to be just waiting for us to slip up to put us in our places. There was a rumor that she was getting married the following year. That would be good, I thought, then she could move out, and have her own children to boss around and leave us alone. We turned our attention to the plates of tasty pigeon-peas cook-up rice before us.

That night during story time, Jimmy read an interesting story about Anancy and how he pretended to be a girl. I liked the way he said "girl," not like us, we said "gyurl." I decided I would try to say some of my words like Jimmy. He was from Antigua. When it was my turn, I read the story of how Anancy outsmarted his children and ended up with more to eat than anyone else. It was my favourite. Our evening came to an end with Aunt Mildred's call: "Okay now, it's bedtime. All the bed-wetters put up your hands." I raised my hand sheepishly. "What! Girl you still wetting bed at 10! You have to sleep on the floor! Cousin Jane when you coming tomorrow you must bring a crapaud so we can tie it to her foot. Is high time this girl stop this bed wetting!"

I didn't mind sleeping on the floor too much. I had company. The thought of a frog tied to my leg scared me though… "Connie gyurl, you tink Cousin Jane gon' bring de crapo tomorrow? "I friken! I hope she fuhget!"
"Well gyurl she say if when she come tomorrow I still suckin' me finga she gon' put bitta aloes 'pon it."
"The two of you be quiet and go to sleep!" Aunt Mildred's voice put an end to our conversation. I closed my eyes, twisting and turning to find a comfortable position on thin

sheets that were spread over the hard, wooden floor. The cool night air came in through the skylight. Why did they make houses with a window too high for anyone to look through, I wondered? As I tried to think about sleep, images of someone sneaking in through that very window near the ceiling kept coming into my mind. I closed my eyes tight, twisted and turned on the floor, and willed myself to ignore the pain in my lower abdomen. I knew I should get up and go to the toilet, but I was too afraid. I had read in a story book about counting sheep ... One... two... three... four...

July 22, 1972

The day didn't start so well, Diary. I wet the bed again! I was so ashamed. Aunt Mildred was her usual self, making me feel worse than I already did...

A rough, angry hand shaking my shoulder awakened me the next day. Aunt Mildred ordered me to the bathroom as she repeated her threat to have Cousin Jane bring a crapaud to tie to my leg at bedtime. I slunk downstairs with my soiled bedding, trying not to make eye-contact with anyone else, but making sure to say my good mornings to everyone loud and clear so as not to incur any additional wrath.

Because it was the genip season, we had to keep an eye on the tray of genips at the front gate and sell to the neighbourhood children. A handful for a cent, a big bunch for five cents, a small basin for twenty-five cents, a large basin for a dollar. Even though we could eat some of the genip Granny had put out for sale, we had to do so in moderation. We had to take care too, to make sure the neigbourhood boys didn't outsmart us. Jimmy Collins always insisted on tasting before buying,

"Leh me taste fus an' den I gon' buy!"

And then nine times out of ten he would say he wasn't buying because the genips were sour. Sometimes Marvin or one of the other cousins would have to chase him down the street to recover what he owed them for the bunches of genips he had gorged. Then there were those like Jason Wilson who never had enough money. "Y'all, trus' me five cents genip nah? Ah guh bring de money tomorrow." We couldn't take those chances because if the money didn't look right, we were in big trouble with Granny.

Between sales we played our favourite games. We girls played Chinese skipping while the boys played marbles. I soon got tired of "Chiney" because I couldn't jump as high as the others. I made my way over to the boys and asked to join their game.

"Yuh gat a taw?" Marvin asked.

When I returned with my big, iron marble all the boys wanted to know how I had acquired it.

"Wha'! Gyurl whey you get dis iron taw from?"

The boys were impressed with my iron marble. That is what the boys in our area used to use to play marbles.

"Daddy bring it home from work fuh me," I declared with

pride. It was easy to get iron ball bearings from the Bauxite Company.

"Gyurl yuh making we kuru seed look like stupidness!"

"Come man, y'all gi' me a game nah?" I really wanted to be a part of the boys' marble game.

"Tomorrow," Marvin answered. " Is four o'clock. We ga' a go upstairs fuh tea."

I knew it wasn't yet four o'clock. They were just envious of my iron taw. I flounced away and stomped up the stairs into the kitchen.

July 23, 1972

Today is Sunday. We went to church, rested and made plans for our big day tomorrow!

After the concert on Saturday night, it was hard to get up on Sunday morning at 6 for 7 o'clock church. We had to get up though. Sunday was church, whether we liked it or not. Going to church was filled with traditions and rituals, most of which I did not understand. I dared not raise any questions, though. Even though I envied my older cousins who got to wear their mantillas because they were confirmed, I was happy I didn't have to starve until after service. We younger ones had two breakfasts on Sundays. We had a little bread and tea before going to church and then later, we joined everyone else in the big Sunday breakfast when we got home. Hot beef or fish stew with fresh home-made bread was the usual Sunday morning fare, along with orange juice and corn flakes. By the time we were finished we could hardly move. Sunday was a long day. It was not a day for playing. We had to sit quietly and read. When I realised that my cousins were all either napping or engrossed in their storybooks, I got my diary out of my suitcase and started writing.

The day went by slowly and the anticipation of the adventure we had planned for the next day made it difficult for me to sleep that night. I lay there thinking about all we would do the next day and imagining the taste of the food we would cook.

July 24, 1972

_Dear Diary, we had a lot of fun today! We had a bush cook in the garden. Mmh! I can still taste the curry..._We completed our chores hurriedly and made our way into the garden. The clearing between the mango and star-apple trees was perfect. While Marvin dug the hole, Fiona, Connie and I gathered dried twigs, sticks and bits of paper and placed them on top of the charcoal in the hole. Garfield then placed a few stones around the hole to finish off the fire-side.

Pam, Hazel and Wendy, our older cousins, were doing the actual cooking. I watched intently as they fried up the beef with onions and garlic. The powerful odor of curry powder, massala and other seasonings filled the air. I was ready to eat even before the food was done, especially when I saw Pam throw some pieces of green mango along with the mango seed into the pot. It took everything in me to control my salivary glands. Everything seemed to be going fine. We kept fanning the fire to make sure it didn't go out and the stew was simmering nicely. I wonder why the potatoes were taking so long to cook. Wendy kept opening the pot every few minutes to check them. Just as she was about to open it again, a scuffling sound made me look up. Garfield, with mischief written all over his face, was trying to make good on his threat to throw a brick into the pot and Hazel was making sure he didn't.

"Y'all ain't know yuh does got to throw a brick in de pot or de bush cook doan be sweet?" he shouted.

Hazel shut the pot quickly and she and Pam stood guard over the area. A few minutes later we were sitting below the trees, feasting on our meal of curried beef with potatoes and white rice! The only thing I found wrong with the meal was that there wasn't enough for me to have more.

Chantal got up and placed her diary on the dresser. She couldn't believe so much time had passed. She was so engrossed in her reading that she had neglected to continue with her sorting and packing. She would have to read again later when she was less busy. As she sorted through books, papers, clothing and other possessions, she reflected on the memories she had recorded so many years ago. Her childhood had been rich with wonderful experiences that had helped to mold her into the person she had become. She marvelled at how well she had documented the sights, smells, sounds and feelings she had experienced as a child. After a few hours of packing, she made herself comfortable in her living-room sofa and continued to re-live her childhood adventures.

July 29, 1972

Well, today was a great day! I finally learned to ride a bike! [...]

Fiona could not believe that at ten years old I still could not ride a bicycle. So, she decided to teach me.
"Look, I gon hol' up de bike an' you pedal an' keep de handle straight, straight."

I started off, wobbling a bit at first. Fiona's hand steadied the bike and I started going more steadily. I was riding! All of a sudden, I no longer felt Fiona's steady hand on the seat. The bike started wobbling uncontrollably! "Fi-i-o-o-n-a!" I screamed as I went crashing to the ground. When she took the bicycle off me and helped me up I felt something warm running down my arms and legs. I had bruised my knees and elbows. Granny gave me a cup of sugar-water to drink and put iodine on my bruises, and said consolingly, "Well, girl it's all in the game. You have to fall down and get up and fall down and get up until you learn." She was right. Before the end of that week, I was riding on my own. I was even practicing to ride with one hand like Aunt Mildred - back straight, head held high, one hand on the handlebar and the other on my thigh. That's what the ladies did to ensure that the wind did not blow their skirts or dresses as they rode.

August 7, 1972

Dear Diary, today is August Monday. We always go to the fair on August Monday... .

The first Monday in August was always a special day. It was Emancipation Day, a day to celebrate freedom. Mostly we enjoyed our own freedom celebration on that day. We did not have to do chores and, provided we behaved well, we went to the August fair at Burnham Park. My friend Darlene and I would meet there and have fun playing, eating and enjoying ourselves on the rides. I was so overjoyed about going to the fair, I didn't cry out when Aunt Mildred tugged at my hair as she combed it.

Along with our older cousins, we made our way to the fair. I had two dollars. I was rich! I would buy ice cream, cake, rock-crest, mauby, go for a ride on the ferris wheel and on the merry-go- round... We met Darlene and her brother just inside the gate. Then off we went to try out the goodies and games. The new attraction this year was a huge ferris wheel. By the time we had had our fill of goodies, Fiona, Darlene, Connie and I had plucked up enough courage to join the line for a ride on that gigantic wheel. I could hear my heart beating as I sat between my two cousins while the man who operated the wheel strapped us in. "Whee!" We were off... We relaxed and chatted elatedly as the wheel began to circle, slowly at first. Then the pace increased. Faster and faster it went. Our chatter ceased. We clutched one another's hands in fear.

"Stop! I want to come out!" Connie screamed.

"Ow Mummy! Help!" That was Fiona. I didn't dare open my mouth. Everything I had eaten was in my throat. As the tears streamed down my face, I prayed silently for the wheel to stop. Even before it came to a halt, the retching started. I made up my mind there and then that that had been my first and last ferris wheel ride! My nice new culotte was soiled. My head and stomach ached. I wanted to go home. The next day, Jimmy, Winslow and the other boys teased us mercilessly. They had ridden the ferris wheel over and over again and had thoroughly enjoyed themselves.

I am ready to go home, Dairy. Today was no fun! We did not get to go to the fair...

"We should protest!"

"Like they forget is Emancipation Day!"

"Schuups! She de Aunty Mildred does fret me!"

"She and the man ain't even married yet and she want we fuh call he 'uncle!'"

My cousins' voices brought me back from to the present. Aunt Mildred had convinced Granny that we had not behaved well enough to deserve our annual treat of going to the fair. Her 'boyfriend' had come to take her to the cinema. Winslow invited him in and then shouted, "Aunty Mildred, Mr. Hendy come to see you!"

She had called him into the bedroom and upbraided him, first for shouting, and also for saying 'Mr. Hendy', instead of Uncle Clyde. As they were heading out, we bade them farewell with, "Bye, bye Aunty Mildred, bye bye Uncle Clyde." A soft "Mr. Hendy", though, followed Jimmy's Uncle Clyde! Our peals of laughter were soon silenced when Aunt Mildred came back into the yard and ordered us all into the house, telling us she would deal with us later. I hated having to sit indoors all day on a day like today when I should have been all dressed up and out at the fair having fun with my cousins and friends! I wanted my mother to come to take me home.

....

August 17, 1972

We spent the day in Glasgow at Cousin Jane, today. Diary, my teeth are still on edge from all the green mangoes I ate today...

Granny, Gramps and the other grown-ups had gone to a funeral on the Corentyne and they had left us with Cousin Jane. Cousin Jane lived at Glasgow in an old cottage, in a big yard filled with mango trees. She had no children and she allowed us to pick and eat as many mangoes as we wanted. We were elated!

"We gon have a mango feas' today!"

Connie and Fiona loved ripe mangoes. They licked the sticky, yellow juice that trickled down their arms and continued sucking on the juicy, ripe mangoes. I didn't like the ripe ones though. Ever since Jimmy had described the way pigs gorged themselves on them, I had stopped eating them. I only ate those that were green or half-ripe. I found my favourite tree, climbed it, settled comfortably between two branches, and ate to my heart's desire. At the end of the day my tongue was blistered and my teeth were numb.

At Cousin Jane's I could climb the trees unhindered. I liked climbing trees. Sometimes I climbed our guava tree at home when Mom wasn't looking. Every so often she would find out what I was up to and I would scramble down as soon as I heard her shouting, "Girl come down from that tree! You playing a tomboy? You want the guavas to get sour? "

Cousin Jane didn't stop me from climbing her trees though. By lunchtime, I was so filled with mangoes I could not do justice to the curried hassar she had prepared. At least I made sure I sucked the sweet curry sauce off the black bones of the fish and ate the potatoes in the sauce. I didn't have room in my stomach for the rice.

"Y'all propa enjoyin' y'all self!" Cousin Jane commented. "The fun comin' to a end soon. Jus' now is back-to-school time!"

Even though I loved school, it would be hard to leave my cousins. I didn't want to be reminded that my vacation was almost at its end.

August 26, 1972

Dear Diary, I came back home today. I was sad to leave my cousins and friends, but Mom had come to take me back. Next week school re-opens and I'll be in a new class! The train ride was different this time. It seems like everything went by too quickly: the steamer ride, the open fields with cows and sheep grazing, the boys playing cricket who looked up and waved as we passed by, the women selling fish and bread at the Mahaicony train station... As I sat in the train lost in the memories of another wonderful Berbice vacation, I tried to remember all the details: the journey, the greetings, the games, learning to ride...

But really, Dear Dairy, I have them all here. I can look back at them throughout the year until my next visit!

"This is how it all started," Chantal said as she closed the book. She remembered the excitement she felt on the return train ride as she tried to tell her mother about all the things that had happened and the fact that she had been able to write them down in her diary. She had turned to her and said, "Mummy, I know what I will be when I grow up. I will be a writer and I will write my life story." Her mother had smiled and told her that she had a lot more living to do. Indeed, she had lived and experienced much more in the past thirty-something years since she said those words. Since then, too, she had set out to do what she had said way back then. She got up and walked over to the suitcase that held the things she was definitely taking with her on her big move overseas. Finally, she had the missing link! Chantal Simmons placed the diary in the folder that held the unfinished manuscript she hoped to complete and publish as soon as she settled into her new life.

AMEENA GOES HOME

Ameena peered out the window trying to catch the last glimpses of her city. She brushed away tears as she sought to make sense of the hazy silhouette of the maze of streets and buildings way down below. From the plane's height, New York didn't look like home. It looked more like something she would read about in books.

She hadn't wanted to leave home. She did not really want to make this trip to Guyana, but it was the first time she was travelling all by herself. So in a way, she was excited. This Summer would not be what she had hoped for: no going to camp with her friends, no swimming lessons, no trips to the beach and Coney Island. Her parents had tried hard to convince her that her visit 'back home' would be an adventure in itself. She wasn't so sure...

What was so adventurous about being bitten by mosquitoes and being in stifling heat all day long? She wasn't even sure if they had Wi-Fi down there. Her parents and their friends from 'back home' were always reminiscing about how it was when they were children, running around all day playing. She found it hard to understand life without a T.V but they made it sound like the coolest thing ever. She was sure they were really bored but were just trying to make their childhood sound like something out of a story book because to them everything about the past was better. In reality, the way her parents spoke about 'back home,' was a mixture of a peaceful paradise, too good to be true and a place with hardships she couldn't understand, like frequent power outages and food shortages. Then there were the mosquitoes. She knew they were plentiful because her mother had packed two large cans of OFF in her suitcase, telling her to remember to spray it on frequently.

"I don't want them mosquitoes over there to eat you alive. Put this on and make sure to always sleep under the mosquito net."

"Guyana!" she mumbled. "Why do I have to go? Why couldn't Grandpa and Grandma come here?" She was only four the last time she visited her grandparents eight years ago so she really didn't remember much about being there. "Anyway," she thought, "at last I have my own phone! I hope I'm able to use it. Although it's not going to be the same like being right there with them, I will still be able to keep up with what's going on with my friends through WhatsApp and Instagram. But what if they don't have Wi-Fi there? This phone will just be a waste... Guyana is in the Third World, right? Her teachers always showed them pictures and videos about how hard life was in those Third-World countries." She sighed and looked out the window. The fluffy white clouds floating by soon took her resentment with them. She gazed out into what looked like the thick layers of snow that cover everything after a Brooklyn snow storm. The difference was that this sea of white stretched out as far as she could see. She couldn't believe her eyes. They were flying above the clouds!

What if she was bored staying for six weeks with two old people? What if the cousins her Mom told her about were mean? What if she couldn't talk to her parents or friend for six whole weeks...?   "Are you okay, honey?" The flight attendant must have seen the worried expression on her face. She gave her a pair of head phones and showed her which channels were for music and which was for the movie. This was so cool! She played around listening to different kinds of music, then watched the movie *Peter Rabbit*. It was so funny. She laughed out loud quite a few times. At first, she was self-conscious but when she realised that everyone else was either laughing too or sleeping, she relaxed and enjoyed the movie. Before she knew it, the plane touched down on the tarmac. They had arrived!

A gust of moist heat enveloped her as she stepped out of the plane. She was the last passenger to leave because she had to wait for the flight attendant to accompany her.
"Praise the Lord, you reach safe my chile!" Aunty Rose smothered her with a warm hug and wet kisses on her cheek. Ameena felt as though she was drowning in a sea of talcum powder, perfume and light sweat. It was hard to believe that she was younger than her mother. She had a large patch of gray in the front of her hair and her lipstick looked as though she had slapped it on hurriedly.

"Girl look how tall you get! You almost bigger than your Grandpa now!" Grandpa stepped forward, gave her a quick peck on her forehead, picked up her suitcase and started heading toward the parking lot.

As they made their way to her grandparents' home, Ameena's attention was divided between trying to keep up with responding to questions about her parents, school and what she would like to do during her time here and the scenery. Everything was so different! The houses, the narrow streets, the way her grandfather had to keep swerving from time to time to avoid potholes, cyclists, or the cows and other animals that wandered into the roadway... She tried to snap some pictures with her phone. So this was the 'home' her Mom and Dad always talked about, she thought. They always made it sound so exciting and special. To her it was all just a jumble of wooden houses built up high, overgrown grass, trees, and hot, blazing sun and mosquitoes that were already trying to feast on her arms and legs.

Ameena stepped through the door that her grandpa held open. After Grandma had finished smothering her with warm hugs and kisses, Carlton and Camille, Aunty Rose's twin, greeted her with bashful hugs and smiles. They looked like they were about her age. She made her way deeper into the house and a familiar rich, warm, rich smell wrapped it self around her and lovingly drew her into the kitchen. She knew immediately what was awaiting her for lunch, her favourite dish of pepperpot. Grandma's pepperpot tasted even better than her mother's. She savoured the rich, sweet, black meaty sauce and eagerly sucked on all the bones. She realised that her grandparents were trying hard to make her welcome and comfortable.

On entering the bedroom that would be hers for the next six weeks, she couldn't help noticing that the curtains and sheets were her favourite colour - lilac. The small bed was neatly made up and a fluffy brown and white stuffed puppy peered out at her from between the pillows. She felt like she had seen it somewhere before. As she stood there wondering, her grandmother came in, picked it up and held it out to her, "You remember him, Meena? It's Bubba. He was your favourite toy the last time you were here. He went everywhere with you. If he wasn't in the bed, you won't fall asleep." Ameena stroked his hair and rubbed her face against his. Yes, there was something familiar about the way the soft, fluffy hair felt against her face. Even though she had outgrown her stuffed toys, she somehow felt that it would be nice to keep Bubba in her bed.

That evening they had dinner at Aunty Rose's. "Do you want to play a game with us?" Carlton asked when they were done eating. She followed them into the living room and stopped in disbelief. "You have a PlayStation?" This is so cool! They had all her favourites: *Knowledge is Power, Sparc, Trials Fusion...*

That night as she climbed into bed, Grandma came and tucked her in. She kissed her goodnight and made sure the netting was tucked in tight around the bed so no mosquitoes would make their way inside. As she lay there thinking about the fun she had had playing with her cousins earlier that evening and all the wonderful things they were telling her they would do for the next six weeks - a day at the creek, visits to the seawalls, zoo and Botanical Gardens... It all sounded so different, but it seemed like it would be fun. She smiled, hugged Bubba close and settled into bed. The rustling of the coconut palms in the cool breeze and the tin-tin of raindrops on the metal roof lulled her to sleep. Ameena was home.

THE REPAST

Boysie looked around in amazement as he followed his good friend Cyril into the community centre hall. The hall was decked out with tables covered with white tablecloths. A cheery, floral centerpiece adorned each table. To one side of the room a D.J dished out soft, soulful tunes; while on the other side warm, rich aromas wafted out from the large, shiny receptacles.

"Boy , yuh sure dis is the right place?" he asked Cyril.

"Dis look more like a wedding set-up than a funeral to-do."

Cyril laughed, "Boy we turnin' foreign! Dis is how dey does do it in New York. Is a repas."

Boysie brushed off some invisible specks of lint from his faded gaberdine pants and tried to smooth the wrinkles in his shirt before following his friend to an empty table. He and Cyril were used to frequenting wakes and nine-nights in the villages nearby, but this was a new experience. He had been a little reluctant to go along this time, not because he didn't know the deceased or her family - that was not usually a reason to keep them from showing up at a wake - but the death announcement had said that after the funeral there would be a repast at the community centre hall. In recent times he had heard them mention repasts in a few other announcements, but he had never been to one. At wakes and nine-nights you would sit in the yard or under the bottom-house and play cards and dominoes and enjoy the rum and ole talk. There would be food yes, some channa or cook-up rice, or fried fish but nothing like the lavish spread he was seeing here. When they sat down, Cyril whispered to him that the deceased, Ms. Maisie, had been a nurse at Fort Wellington hospital before migrating to the States for many years and all the children lived over there but they had brought her home because she would always say, "Carry me back to Guyana and bury me in my Hopetown mud."

Boysie watched the people as they streamed in and took their seats. He wondered how many of them were like him. Two other villagers joined them at their table. They were loud in their praise for the deceased and her children. Ms. Maisie would be really proud of how the girls give her a good send-off they said. As he listened intently, Boysie learned that the big, new concrete house on the main road near the gas station was the house Maisie had built because she planned to spend the Winter months back home after she retired. Sadly, however, she didn't even get to enjoy the house because she suffered a massive heart attack just as she was packing up to come home. He heard them talk about her husband Robbie and how one of them big cranes you does see on T.V crushed him in a building he was working on doing tile work. The girls, they said, pointing them out, were all doing well - one was a nurse, another an engineer and the baby girl was a lawyer. Boysie sipped on his beer and munched on the patties and cheese straws someone had brought over to the table. Every now and again he would chime in with a "Hmm... Yuh huh... dat nice... so sad..."

Soon the Minister arrived and said a prayer. After they served the family, everybody else could form a line to get their food. When his turn came and he went up, Boysie could not believe his eyes... curry chicken, fried rice, roti, cook-up rice, fried fish, stew fish, baked chicken... there was food galore and it all smelled so good! He decided he would sample a little bit of everything. He stepped back to the table gingerly, making sure to hold on carefully to his almost-overflowing plate.

"Boysie, boy, yuh alright deh?" Cyril called out to him from behind his mountain of food. All Boysie could do was give a gleeful nod as he loosened his belt and settled down to enjoy the meal. As the evening went on, he found himself joining in more actively in the conversation:

"Yes, man, dese gyurls really do dey mudda proud today!"

At eight-thirty, Boysie reminded Cyril that they had to get home before nine. As they were leaving, he went over to the table where the family was sitting. "Thank you, Misses. Y'all did a very nice thing here for yuh Mudda. She was a very nice, kind nurse. I remember her from when I was in de hospital. All o' us in de village gon' miss her."

He and Cyril parted ways at the line top. He began walking briskly toward his house but a sharp pain cut through the middle of his stomach and slowed him down. He limped along, rubbing his stomach and belching. He wondered if he had any ginger in the house. That would take care of his stomach pain. As he fumbled to open the door, the clock started chiming the nine o'clock hour. He almost tripped on the rug as he hurried over to the radio and turned it on. He couldn't afford to miss the death announcements. Maybe there would be another repast soon.

INTERLUDE I

Abby ran a well-manicured hand through her hair and lowered her sunglasses unto her nose. As she closed her eyes and settled more comfortably into her beach chair, the northeast trades brought to her ear the question that would cause everything to change: "May I join you?

The tide came in and swept them out to sea on a wonderful ride...

Ten years, seven children and two hundred and seventy-five pounds later, she plopped herself down on the sofa at the end of the day. Her tired, wrinkled hands reached for the remote. Her favourite show was on. She loved to watch Xiomara and lose herself in her adventures and escapades. She was young, beautiful, talented and street-smart too! No man could run rings around her.

Today she was on the beach lounging in her lilac beach chair. As she lowered her sunglasses on her nose and closed her hazel eyes, a handsome young man strolled over and asked, "May I join you?"

And even though every fiber in her being willed her to get up and leave the room, Abigail Small sat, glued to her chair and watched with incredulity as her heroine, Xiomara, blushed, lifted her hazel eyes and welcomed the handsome stranger with a smile.

WHY, MA?

The stifling heat reflects off the tin roof of the church unto my body. My handkerchief provides little relief. I sit here conflicted. Should I rejoice or be sad? The huge pew seems to swallow us, the seven children of the deceased.

"Dearly beloved we are gathered here this afternoon to mourn the passing of our dear brother James …"

Dear brother my foot! The last time my father had set foot in a church must have been 25 years ago on his wedding day…

The preacher drones on and I observe my siblings. My two older brothers, Marlon and Kevin, are trying their best to sit up straight in their stiffly starched, white cotton shirts but it is clear that they're struggling to stay awake. Every now and again their heads droop forward and then spring back up. Abena, Arianne and Akima, the three youngest, can't seem to stop fidgeting. They had been excited to make this secret trip to the city and now could not understand why they were being made to sit quietly in a church, surrounded by people they didn't know.

I had left our home, in that dusty, old town up the Demerara River the previous day and was only aware of these recent developments when Akima, the youngest, ran up to me at our aunt's house as we were preparing to leave for the church and announced gleefully, "Alana t'ief we 'way from

Ma and bring we to town!" Alana was trying her best to pay attention to the service and at the same time control the three young ones. She, the eldest, felt that it was right for us all to be there to say a final farewell to our father.

"James Joaquin was a good man, a loving father, a good provider ..."

Good provider? Hmm... I guess he must have got that story from Alana. She always talks of the days when our father held down a good job and had enough extra money to buy us gifts and treats. She remembers too, the days of having orange juice, corn flakes and bacon and eggs on Sunday mornings. I must have been too young to remember...

"Our sympathy goes out to the family of James, to his grieving wife and ..."

Ma must be beside herself right now. She must be livid that Alana had defied her orders and brought the little ones to the city.

"Y'all big ones can go if y'all want, but leave these children here!" Those were her words when she realised that we were determined to travel to the city for the funeral. She wanted nothing whatsoever to do with this event.

She must have made the house more secure when she realised that she was all alone. Jumping at the slightest sound as she peered through the cracks in the curtains. Looking out to see whether my father would come sneaking up the stairs.

You see, my mother did not believe that my father was really dead. She was not even with us that Sunday afternoon because, in her mind, it was a trap he was laying for her and she would not be caught! So she sat and she waited. And as the hot, sticky afternoon turned into a stormy night, she must have worked herself up to such a frenzy that she screamed at us as we walked in at nine that night drenched to the bone. "Is where y'all coming from at this hour? And 'Lana, I didn't tell you not to take these children out of this house? Y'all father got y'all with a lot o' nonsense!"

My mother was changing before our eyes. She hardly laughed and the slightest thing set her off. As I watched her transform before my eyes, I tried hard to hold on to glimpses of her former vibrant self. She was the one who, in those days before television, would organise our family concerts and outings. "Come on now," she'd say with excitement. "It's Saturday night. Time to get creative!" We'd all perform. The children and Ma, that is. It would all be going so well until we heard the sound of the gate opening and heavy boots pounding up the stairs. A blanket of fear would descend, bringing an end to the festivities. We knew what greeting to expect, we had heard it so often, "Everybody having fun until the big, bad wolf arrive, eh!"

The big, bad wolf. That is what he became on a Saturday night after a day of drinks with "the boys" at the market square, or at Scrabby Rum-Shop. Sometimes he brought company home with him. Then he had my mother and brothers scurrying around at his beck and call. "Marlon and Kevin, come boys, come set up the drinks. Annie get some cutters fuh de boys."

Maybe the preacher was right. Maybe he had been a good provider at some point. We owned our own home, we were always well dresssed - no Bata yatching boots or rubber dinkies for us! It was tetrex uniform and Clarks shoes. He had even bought an old Ford Corsair with which he drove us to school (never mind we had to give it a push-start most mornings). What had happened? Why had my father changed so much?

Alana always blamed the Company for retrenching him. She said that if he had not lost his job with the Company, things would have been different. I'm not so sure about that. If he had indeed been better, I blamed the company he kept for the change in him. I detested those men who only came over to drink rum, talk about politics and gossip. *Didn't they have anything better to do? Why spend so many hours after work or during the day sitting idly in a beer garden in the marketplace or in somebody's house?*

Alana said that she was sorry for Dad. He had become insecure. He was no longer the main breadwinner. As a free-lance mason, he earned much less money so it was mostly Ma's salary that kept the family going. According to her, that is the reason we were able to maintain that standard of living. I still had my doubts. *But, I guess she did have a valid*

point about him being insecure... But why would a man allow his
insecurities to drive him to such a state though…?

Ma would bustle around the kitchen, frying the fish and preparing boiled channa for "the boys".Usually, it was well past midnight, but she had to stay up until they were done, just in case they needed something more and of course, to clear away and wash up after they had finished.

As I look at her now, it's hard for me to come to grips with my mother's illness. She was always so busy: awake at the crack of dawn, cooking, baking, cleaning, busy in the garden, busy helping us with our homework, busy at her job, busy with church activities. Now, at only seventy, she seemed decades older. Now all I could find was a faint shadow of the beautiful, intelligent woman I knew and loved in the person lying in fetal position on her bed whimpering, unable to sleep, afraid of being left alone, the ability to contain bodily waste gone …

It didn't seem like that long ago that she would dress up and go out with her friends to have a good time. Like that Boxing Day when she went to the ladies' social dressed in her lilac, linen pants suit. The peplum top accentuated her tiny waist; the pants hugged her ample hips and then fell gracefully to just above her high-heeled sandals. When she came back, she tried her best to respond to all our questions as she shared with us, not only the excitement of her outing but also some of the goodies she brought tucked in her purse.

"Ma, they really played calypso music at the party?
"Show us again how Ms. Jones danced to 'Congo Man.'"
"Is Ms. Margo make this cheese roll, nuh? They melting in my mouth."
We all jumped and fell silent at the sound of the door slamming shut and the louvres rattling. We were so busy enjoying ourselves we had not heard the gate or the sound of Dad's footsteps ascending the stairs. He took one look at Mom, pushed her against the wall and yelled, "Is where you been in that tight, tight pants?
"Ladies' social? Is who you think you fooling? And is who dance with you?" He wasn't really interested in listening to her answers. He had come in looking for a fight. We disappeared into our bedrooms. Abena, Akima and I huddled together in the closet hugging each other and crying inconsolably. We knew exactly what was taking place outside. We clung to each other tighter as we heard the sound of glass breaking.

Then I heard my mother say something I was hoping she would have said a long time ago. "I refuse to take this anymore," she declared. "I'm leaving." I was elated! I knew she would take us with her. I guess we would go to stay with Aunty Mavis who lived in the Big Shot area. Her husband had a big job with the Company and they had no children. I imagined myself going to school on that special bus with my friend Desa and all the other managers and supervisors' children. Akima, Abena and I lay in bed making whispered plans about what we would do when we moved to those tranquil surroundings.

I had arisen early the next morning, filled with nervous excitement. Maybe my mother would wait until my father left to make her move. I had decided that I would get a head start and start putting together my clothes and toys.

My hopes were dashed when I stepped into the living room and saw my parents cuddling. Dad was apologising profusely and promising to do better. Confused, I tiptoed back into my room, crawled back into bed and pulled the covers tightly over my head. The whole situation was too baffling for me. I just couldn't understand what had made her change her mind.

They went shopping later that day and she returned with a beautiful, gold lamé evening gown. She wore it when they went out dancing to ring in the New Year, but nothing really changed. In fact, the insecurities Alana spoke about became more pronounced as time went by.

On one of the regular late night drinking sessions in our living room the topic seemed to be women and the importance of maintaining control over them.
"Boy you does really got to keep these women in their place!"
"I know what you mean, partner. You see what happen with

Charlie? He let the woman take charge of too many things. She bringing in the big money, doing all the shopping and paying the bills. Before he know it, she kick he out and bring in another man!"

"That would never happen to me" my father's voice boomed loudly above the murmurs and exclamations of his buddies. "Not me! She don't dare! Over my dead body!"

Was he afraid of what he had heard about Charlie? Whatever the case was, the situation seemed to grow worse with accusations of infidelity and poisoning and the like flying left and right on almost a daily basis. Ma had had to leave her job. Her blood pressure was consistently high. The spark in her eyes grew dimmer and dimmer. She jumped at the slightest sound.

When they told her he had collapsed at the market square and they had taken him to the hospital, she thought he was up to one of his tricks. So she didn't bother to waste her time going to the hospital. She knew he was trying to trap her. Then she heard that his sister had come and taken him down to the hospital in the city for better treatment. They were all in it together. His family had never liked her anyway. Then there was Alana now telling her about his funeral! She had always been his favourite. Somehow he must have roped her into his plans. And she had the face to take these little children all the way to the city just to play along with him!

The days became weeks, the weeks, months, the months, years…

"He must have gone to Canada," she would say. He had long wanted to go there but his sisters had said they couldn't take the burden of him and all those children…

And so, on that hot July afternoon as I sat in the church, I decided to be happy - happy that my mother's years of torment and abuse were finally over. My happiness was short-lived, however, when I reflected on what the years of physical, verbal and emotional abuse had done to her.

Eventually, many years later, Ma asked me to accompany her to the N.I.S Office. "Good morning Mrs. Joaquin. How may I help you?" "I'm here to see if I could receive Survivor's Benefits."

"Do you have the Death Certificate?" She handed it to the clerk.

"Name: James Joaquin. Date of death: July 8, 19…, but Mrs. Joaquin, why only now? Your husband died 10 years ago!" "I had to be sure," she replied, glancing around nervously. "I had to be sure he wasn't coming back."

The stifling heat reflects off the tin roof of the church unto my body. My handkerchief provides little relief. We sit here -

the children, grandchildren and great-grandchildren of the deceased. We occupy three huge pews.

"Dearly beloved. We're gathered here today to mourn the passing of our sister, Anne Joaquin."

Today, I attend the funeral of a woman whose life ended way too early, many years ago. Today, I sit here, and I know how I feel. Today, I sit in this hot church on a steaming Sunday afternoon and the tears flow silently as the voice in my head screams: "Why, Ma? Why didn't you fight back? Why, couldn't we help you more? Why for goodness sake hadn't you left? Why, Ma? Why, why did you allow him to kill you?"

UNE CARTE À MAMAN

Ma chère Maman,

I salute you in the language you taught me to love. The language of romance, sophistication and adventure. I clung to every word you shared about your elegant teacher Madame Le Blanc and the many adventures you and your classmates had practising French with visitors to the city. I cherish the name you gave me as evidence of your love of that language. And, ma chère Maman, your love helped kindle in me a love of languages and of life. A love that still burns bright.

What an exciting youth you had: singing in choirs, going for rides along the seawall and strolls and picnics in the Promenade Gardens, attending lively dances... What were those steps you spoke about? – 'the twist,' 'lambeth walk,' 'lindy hop'... You did so much when you were young and yet there were some things you were not able to do. How could the daughter of a seamstress and foundry worker realise her dream of becoming a doctor? You never accomplished your own dreams fully, but you made sure that we, your offspring, realised ours.

Wonderful activities filled my own youth: singing in the choir, performing with my school's dance troupe, playing the piano, going on school trips and to school dances... I relished my performances at school events, music festivals and piano recitals. You were always there to cheer me on, even when I got cold fingers and messed up the notes. You made so many sacrifices to make these things possible.

Tonight, I sit on the edge of my bed in an air-conditioned room, thousands of miles away from home, writing this letter to you. I remember the times we spent together in your tiny bedroom. The low, dull hum of the once-brown table fan provided a measure of relief from the afternoon heat and served as the accompaniment to our many conversations.

Do you think your grands and great-grands would understand or appreciate those simple pleasures we took for granted? I wonder... A strange, new creature now takes its place at the table these days. It's oh so needy - constantly demanding our attention! What would you think of how this creature we call a cell phone is always at hand?

I'm sure you remember how we used to long for a T.V when we were growing up. We felt so left out of things. It seemed like one by one all our friends were getting T.Vs, everybody but us ... I now see that I have to thank you *Maman*. At least we learned to read and to use our imaginations. Family concerts on weekends and story-telling on black-out and full-moon nights drew us close together. And of course, kneeling with you at your bedside, because you insisted that "a family that prays together, stays together."

I thank you *Maman* for teaching me. I was not a model student but you would be happy to know that I'm finally learning. Believe it or not, *Maman*, as a mother, I am now learning the art of patience and perseverance. Those lessons I learned from observing you, like – you should never give up on your children… How invaluable they have proved to be!

Oh *Maman*! As I look back at the fortitude and dignity with which you bore the pain and shame as one of the beloved fruit of your belly became a public spectacle, I applaud your faith. Despite the excruciating pain you suffered, you never gave up hope and you lived to see him triumph.

Life goes by so quickly! Where did the little girl with thick French twists go? The girl with her flouncy dresses, can-cans and bright ribbon bows – what happened to her? She always wanted to grow up quickly, didn't she? Now *I* know that it happens quickly, oh so quickly, and there's nothing we can do about it.

I hope you understood my imperfect way of showing I cared. I know I did not say it enough… *C'est pourquoi je t'écris cette carte, Maman.* To confirm my love for you. To assure you of my gratitude. To seek forgiveness for my failings. But I know you will never read this letter *Maman*. Time went by too quickly… I never got to tell you one last time… *"Ma chère Maman, je t'aime..."*

Ta fille,

Marie Claire.

HER RING, HER BATTLE

She sat, lost in thought. As she rocked herself gently back and forth, she changed the ring from her second finger, then to the middle, and finally to her index. She frowned as she looked at it on that finger. The old people had always said that "nice" girls should not wear their rings on their index finger, doing so meant they were 'looking out.' "Schuuups!" She sucked her teeth. She had no choice. The ring, her wedding band, no longer fit the ring finger. To tell the truth, the only times it fit were during her periods of pregnancy. Even when she had first received it, on her wedding day, it was a size too big. But everybody told her not to worry about it: "Gyurl you gon' soon fatten out an' it will fit."

And even though she did fatten out; after six babies the ring still was not her fit.

"Sister D, look you lef' yuh piece o' wire on de kitchen counta." She smiled as she thought of Beulah. She had employed Beulah in the 60s to help her clean up and watch the children while she was at work. Her response to Beulah usually went something like this: "Yes Beulah, you just give me my piece o' wire! It's mine! My husband gave it to me on our wedding day." Beulah had been with them for many years, until the children grew up. Now, though she was taking care of her own grandchildren and Agatha was Sister D's caregiver.

The ring Beulah used to call her "piece o' wire" was her prized possession... They were young and in love. The Bible says "it's better to get married than to burn..." so they got married even though they weren't quite ready. He didn't have money for a big, expensive ring. He bought what he could afford, and she was happy. As she sat there reflecting on the past, she removed the ring from the index finger of her left hand and placed it on the ring finger. It slipped off the finger unto the floor and rolled under the china cabinet. As she retrieved it, Agatha offered to put the ring in the jewel case in the bedroom. Sister D's protest was insistent and almost child-like, "No, no! It's my ring! It's mine, mine!" Agatha smiled as she remembered the last time Sister D had been hospitalized. Her son Aubrey had tried to remove the ring from her finger as she lay in a semi-conscious state. He wanted to put it away for safe-keeping. The old lady had clenched her fists tightly. He had to force her fingers open to remove the ring.

"'Gatha, where is my ring?" She was visibly upset on Agatha's next visit to the hospital.

"Sister D, don' worry yourself. Look. I have it here. Aubrey put it in the jewel box. He didn't want you to lose it at the hospital." A look of relief had spread across her face.

They always teased her about that ring. It was all she had now, her only link to him. He had left several years ago, turned his back and headed for greener pastures. But she still had the ring. It reminded her of happier times and of a

promise made fifty year ago: "'til death do us part."
Believing that promises were meant to be kept, she had
always tried her best to live by those words and those in the
marriage vows too... "For better, for worse, for richer, for
poorer, in sickness and in health..."

His heavy smoking and family history of bronchial problems
had landed him in the hospital on several occasions. She
lovingly nursed him back to health. She couldn't afford to be
sick in those days. She was a wife, mother, nurse,
superwoman... There were many months when he was
without a job and she was the sole breadwinner. How could
she be sick? She just had to keep going.

He always had a restless spirit, even in the early days when
they were young and in love. He was always looking for
betterment.
"D, girl I hear 'bout this job at sea. They need a technician.
They paying really well. If I go and work with them for two
years that will set us right! We can buy our own house."
So off he went to sea. And after being away for six months,
he was back with wonderful tales that fascinated the
children, about life in those far-away places. A few years
later he was itching to leave again.
"D, if you give me a divorce and I go to the States, I could do
a business marriage and then me and you could marry
over after I get fix up and divorce the yankee woman. Then
you and the children can come and live in the States. It will
only take a few years."

She had put her foot down there! NO divorce! Divorce was not a word in her vocabulary - "'til death do us part!"

Determined to seek greener pastures, he approached her a few years later with a more reasonable proposal.

"D, love, I hear they need skilled workers in Canada. Let's apply to go. We'll go as a family. Seeing that you're a nurse and I am a technician, we should get through." She decided to support him with this scheme. There was a flurry of activity: filling forms, receiving the appropriate immunization and the like. Then came the interview. She was never quite sure what went wrong there. Maybe it was the size of their family – six children. The people probably couldn't imagine them being able to support such a large family without public assistance. Or, maybe he had just "wrong-talked." The Canadian official looked over his horn-rimmed glasses and asked, "So, Sir, what do you hope to achieve by migrating to Canada?"

"I would like to spend enough time there to accumulate enough funds so that I could return home and live comfortably when I retire," was Alvin's confident response. One month later the letter arrived: "… we regret to inform you that your application to migrate to Canada has been rejected…"

They were all disappointed. She was not the type to wallow in her sorrow though. She consoled her family with "the Lord knows best" and kept busy in her many roles – night-duty at the hospital, day-duty at home, cleaning, cooking, washing, ironing, gardening, giving neighbour Joan's husband his insulin, dressing Ms. Annie's sore foot, suturing Rover's wounds whenever he got into fights with the neighbourhood dogs, helping the children with their homework, sewing their clothes, going to market…

Sister D stared with unseeing eyes at the document in her hands. "DIVORCE DECREE" it read. Divorce Decree? Divorce Decree? She battled valiantly with the tears that were trying to invade her usual composure.
<<*Alvin! How could you do this? What about 'til death do us part?*>>
As she forced the tears back down, the song that got her through times like these sounded over and over in her head. *"Don't cry out loud…"*

The tears conceded defeat. Instead of dissipating however, they trickled down her trachea and stayed close together waiting for another opportunity …

The painful lump in her throat prevented her from singing but she allowed the song to keep playing in her head,
"…just keep it inside…"
Sister D got up. She folded the document carefully and locked it away in her jewellery box.

'Gatha was concerned. Sister D seemed to be in pain. Her face was contorted, and she held her hand to her throat.

"Sister D why you holding your throat like that? It paining you?"
"I feel as though it has a lump in it. I can hardly swallow." Her voice was laboured as she forced to get the words out. "You must be catching a cold." Gatha responded. I gon' make some warm salt water for you to gargle with and you can sip some lemon and honey later."

The sound of gargling coming from the bathroom woke Angie. Her mother had been having problems with hoarseness and sore throat for some time now. No cold or 'flu, just these throat problems. She would have to suggest a visit to the doctor.

Dr. Nelson examined Dorothy Ross' throat. He thought he saw something, so he referred her to an ENT specialist. The results of the Barium test revealed that something was growing in her throat. So, Dr. Kumar, the specialist, wanted to investigate further to see what it was. A biopsy… "That's enough, Angie! I'm not going back to Dr. Kumar. If something in my throat I don't want to know what it is! I will pray and trust the good Lord that if anything is there it will go. If not, then let me go back to my Maker the way I came, not, with any cut or any part of me missing!"
Angie sighed. She knew it would be futile to try to get her mother to change her mind.

....

Glancing over at her mother, Angie noticed she was playing with the ring again. Since her last stroke – her third - she had lost more weight. The ring no longer fit her ring finger, but she refused to give it up. The only finger it fit snuggly now was the thumb. She was humming and tapping her feet now. The lump in her throat and the pain and hoarseness had long gone. She could hum and sing without any trouble…

"… learn how to hide your feelings…"

Sister D was glad she had not allowed that doctor to cut and probe into her. <<*Faith is a wonderful thing,*>> she thought, <<*it has made me well.*>> That is why she wouldn't lose faith when it came to Alvin. He could be coming home any day now…
"Gatha, you must call and make arrangements with Mr. Ralph for the car?"
"What car, Sister D?"
"We have to go to the airport tomorrow," Sister D replied, "Alvin's coming home."
'Gatha shook her head and sighed, <<*Oh dear. Poor Sister D, still livin' in the past.*>>

In the first five years after his departure he had maintained contact with her. He called, wrote, sent her presents and cards on special occasions, a barrel or two and a "small piece" every now and again. But then his communication became more sporadic.
<<*The children think I don't know. I heard the whispers, though.*

He's living with a white woman in London. But don't worry with him, let him enjoy himself. When dog foot bruk he go' fin' he massa home. Alvin **must** *come back home some day! And when he's ready, I'll be here!>>*

The years came and went but no Alvin. The world didn't have to know her business, though… She always made sure she showed a good face to the public. To the neighbours' compliments on how well she looked, she would smile and say: "Thank you neighbour. You know I
gotta keep myself looking good for when Mr. Ross come home!
"….learn how to hide your feelings."
Even after she received the divorce papers from London, she still lived in hope…

The ring slipped from her finger and rolled over to the other end of the room. Angie was the first to notice that she wasn't wearing it, so she asked 'Gatha.
"Miss 'Gatha you see Mommy ring?" I notice she didn't have it on and I didn't want to ask her. You know how upset she gets over the ring?"
"Girl, the ring keep on fallin' off the other day so I decided to put it up. It in the jewel box on the vanity case."
Angie was surprised. "You mean Mommy let you do that? That's strange. You realise the whole weekend gone by and she ain't ask for her ring? I wonder what's going on with her?"

After their initial defeat 15 years ago, the army of tears had retreated to the trachea, waiting … The constant massaging and praying bothered them. They knew it was a tactic to cause them to desert, to give up the fight. After holding council, they decided that ambush would be a wise strategy. Where should they hide? The gurgling, bubbling gastric juices constantly rose into the trachea to converse with them. They decided that the stomach was as good a place as any to regroup and lay in wait to strike the fatal blow…

Both Angie and 'Gatha had noticed that whenever Sister D ate certain foods she complained of pains in her stomach. On a few occasions she had not been able to keep her meals down. Smaller portions and less spicy foods seemed to be the best way to deal with the problem. As time went by though, the pain became almost unbearable. Sister D's face contorted in pain. She groaned softly and clutched her stomach. On touching her stomach, Gatha encountered a hard, stiff ball. There was hardly any protest when they took her to the hospital, and she was admitted. As she lay there her eyes glazed in pain, the Doctor called Angie aside and said, "Ms. Ross. it's terminal. Your mother has a large mass in her stomach. We suspect it's much more widespread but at her age and with her history of strokes there's nothing we can do now. It must have been growing there for some years now."

Angie tried her best to make her mother's last days as comfortable as possible. Knowing how she had clung to hope about her husband's return, she asked, "Mom, do you want me to call Dad and ask him to come?"
Her mother's tired response surprised her.
"Come? For what?"

And so, the mass that had formed from the union of unshed tears and gastric juices moved in for the kill. It was certain it would make her scream and bawl. This would certainly dissolve and release those tears that had been held at bay for so long. She, however, held fast to her resolve: *"don't cry out loud.."* All the enemy could get out of her were a few weak groans. This made it even more angry. It twisted and yanked on the badly-scared stomach. As the dark bloody substance trickled from her lips Sister D sighed and drew her final breath knowing she had won her war.

THRU' HIS EYES

They say you should look for the good in others. I tried hard to bear this in mind every time I had dealings with Carmen. She was a devil, or a saint, depending on who was describing her.

Sometimes I wondered if it was that she just couldn't help herself. My first encounter with her was some five years ago. It was my first time at Bible Study since moving to the city. She greeted us with a warm smile and welcoming hugs when we entered the room. I liked her immediately. She made me feel so comfortable and at home. Later, we chatted as we stood at the bus stop. She asked the children, "Which school y'all going to?" When they responded, she blurted out, "Oh, Teacher Angela ole school! So she tief up de money an' she gone out de country!" I was flabbergasted! Teacher Angela was my friend and I knew that she had not gone overseas. In fact, she still lived right here in the city. The reason she had left her post as Principal of that school was to take up a more lucrative position at the local office of an international organisation. Why were people so scandalous, I wondered?

Despite that initial experience I found myself in her company constantly and my feelings for her fluctuated between loathing and admiration.
"Gyurl you know wha' Carmen do? She goin' 'round telling people how Junior does smoke ganja." It was evident that

Dorothy was upset by what she had heard about her son. I wondered if Dorothy had her facts straight though. So I asked her if she was sure it was Carmen who had said so. "Sure? I dead sure!" Dorothy retorted. "She talk so much that she even go an' talk wid me cousin and *she* come back an' tell me. I doan know is wha' wrang wid dat girl. She really dangerous!" How could Carmen do something like that?

I was disappointed in her! Yes, the boy was troublesome and rebellious, but no one ever saw him smoking! And to say he was smoking weed! She was slandering the child! I couldn't stop thinking about my conversation with Dorothy. Should I confront Carmen? I couldn't avoid her. She was my Christian sister after all... Just then the phone rang. It was Carmen.
"Eh, eh, girl, leh we talk dis lil name. You hear Maggie gon be a granmudda soon?"
 "Really? You sure?" I inquired tentatively.
"How yuh mean if I sure? Jus' yesterday I see she son an' a gyurl goin' in at Dr. Bacchus. And de girl ve-ery pregnant! Gyurl, I tell you! Sin bearin' blossom! Ha ha!" She laughed. "Anyway, I gone. We gon' talk tomorrow night!"

The news was disturbing. Jermaine was still in high school. I wondered how Maggie was taking it. Maybe that is why she seemed so distracted lately... It took every ounce of self-control I had to stop myself from picking up the phone to call her. Carmen sounded very certain of her information, but I decided that it would be best to wait for Maggie to disclose the news to me herself, when and if she chose to do so.

The next day Maggie, her family and her pregnant *niece* from the interior were all at Bible study. Jermaine had been accompanying his cousin to the doctor's clinic seeing that she was not familiar with the city. For me that was the last straw! I had had it with Carmen! You could never take anything she said at face value! You always had to doctor it with loads of salt! I decided to keep my distance. If my dog was sick, I didn't want her help! She was too scandalous!

Psalm 130: 3 was the verse we focused on in Bible study the following week: *"If errors were what you watch, O Jah, Oh Jehovah, who would stand?"* We were admonished to look for the good in others and not to focus on their shortcomings. I saw that I had something to work on, especially in connection with my attitude toward Carmen, but I was still wary. It was really hard to apply the counsel and I still kept avoiding her. When I saw her coming in one door, I left through the other. For me the Caller's I.D was a blessing. When I realised that the call was from Carmen I refused to pick up the phone; she would get the message soon enough. The following Sunday we heard that Brother Galloway was ill. The Elders were soliciting volunteers to take care of his meals and laundry while he was in hospital. By the time we said the last Amen, Carmen was there with her usual pot-salt self, offering her services. One day, Sylvie stopped over to find out whether I would accompany her.to the hospital to visit Brother Galloway.

"Girl, you know I don't like hospitals." I begged off. "Give Brother Galloway my regards. Tell him I'm praying for his speedy recovery." Later that day, she called me. "Girl, well you know your friend Carmen was very much there at the hospital! Brother Galloway was loud in his praise of her. He says she is always there, three times a day taking good care of him. To him she is a God-send."

Good for him, I thought. It's not like I hadn't seen her kind acts before, but I wondered why she was showing him so much love and attention. She had to be getting something out of this...

Seeing that the children were out of school for the August holidays, we decided to host a party for them. As usual, Carmen was in the thick of things: baking cakes, cooking roti, teaching the children to do the *Cupid Shuffle...*

On our way home from Bible Study one evening Gloria mentioned that she had noticed the way I avoided Carmen. I explained my reason to her. "I don't want to get burnt girl. I prefer to keep her at arm's length."

"Maybe I have to start doing the same, " Gloria said. "You know Dorette had pox a few weeks ago. Well. I heard that she going telling people to be careful how they dealing with my daughter because they got plenty things people does say is pox but it does really be bigger things! You know is what she really mean, right?" Gloria's revelation did not come as surprise, but it still saddened me and I wondered how Carmen always seemed to get the story wrong. I felt justified in my decision to keep my distance from her.

Shortly after I arrived home that night, Sister Alice called. She had seen me leave hurriedly and she had wanted to talk. "You know, Mavis, I notice how you treating Carmen. I think you should really give yourself a chance to get to know her. She really means well but sometimes she's a bit overzealous and she gets the story wrong."

"But Sister Alice, she should know as a Christian that slander is wrong. She should make sure she gets the facts straight before she goes around spreading false stories and casting innocent people in a bad light," I responded impatiently.

"Yes Mavis, you're right. I think that she is getting some help in that regard. You know she has her own problems at home, I can't go into detail, but we should try to bear with her. I have known Carmen since she was a teenager. She's a really kind, loving, helpful person. Her heart is in the right place. Look at how attentive she was to Brother Galloway when he was in hospital. You know last night Lucille's baby was catching fits and if Carmen hadn't gone over to help her, the child might have died! Remember we are all imperfect. She has her faults and we have ours. You know, she's really working on trying to be a better person. I think you should try to see her good side," Sister Alice pleaded with me. I promised her I would try, even though I knew it would be very difficult, if not impossible. Before going to bed that night I decided to look again at Psalm 130:3, *"If errors were what you watch, O Jah. Oh Jehovah, who would stand?"* Was I really imitating Jehovah God by focusing on Carmen's faults? Sister Alice was not the first person who had advised me to look for the good in her. I think Jehovah is really using these ones to speak to me. I know that I want Him to hear my prayers, so I really should forgive Carmen and give her a chance. Even as I prayed that night, I knew that it would take a lot of prayer and much hard work for me to change my attitude toward Carmen.

The sixth of January 2011 is a day I'll never forget. The insistent ringing of the phone demanded that I drag my tired self out of bed. I had tossed and turned for most of the night. A blackout all night long meant that the mosquitoes had had a field day. To top it off, it had been a night devoid of breeze. It was only with the cooling rains and light breezes of the approaching dawn that I had finally fallen into a doze, only to be awakened by the phone. It took a few minutes for me to understand what the person on the other end of the line was saying. They wanted me to come to the morgue to identify a body – they suspected it was my brother. There had been a drive-by shooting the previous night.

The dull throb in my head had now grown into a pounding pain that extended to the back of my neck. I really didn't want to go to that hospital alone. Sylvie had a dentist's appointment, Judy was in bed with a migraine, Sister Alice had to baby-sit her grandchildren... None of my friends was available to accompany me. I wrapped my arms around my body in an attempt to stay warm and control my trembling as I made my way into the hospital compound. All alone, it seemed as if my shoes had lead insoles. "Dear Jehovah God," I prayed, "please see me through this dark time. Please help me to cope."

The two hundred yards from the gate to the morgue seemed like twenty miles. Hesitantly, I approached the door. In that moment, a loving arm, encircled my waist, and an equally warm voice said, "Sis, as soon as I heard, I decided to come to see if I could help. I couldn't let you go through this alone." The tears were streaming down my face as I turned and hugged her. "Thanks Carmen. Thanks!"

Carmen kept her arms around me, and we entered the building together. I thanked God for answering my prayer and I knew that this good side of Carmen was what He saw. It was the side *I* needed to see as well.

INTERLUDE II

She tapped her fingers, swayed in her seat; she sang along to the pulsating beat. His plucking and strumming pulled her heartstrings out. It was easy to dance to the beat of his song. But time went by and she longed for more. His feet, were they as nimble as his fingers? Would he hold her close, glide across the floor; would they rock and jive all through the night?

Just then, she looked up, way across the room. His magnetic strumming drew her in. She had to go. With graceful twirls and hips, a-sway, she obeyed the call of the strings; with outstretched arms, she danced his way. The floor would be theirs!

Her dazzling smile and open arms he just could not resist. The other dancers faded away and the floor, it gladly welcomed them. But, wait! No, this couldn't be! Why the sweaty palms and bungling feet? Why was it so hard to follow his lead?

And so it was that the handsome guitar-man continued to fill the night with his soulful rhythms and way across the room, she danced, oh how she danced!

HELLO, UNCLE SAM!

I couldn't stop pinching myself. Was it really true? Was this really happening? I reached into my handbag and took out my passport. Yes, it was true! After so many years of trying, just when I had all but given up hope, I finally got through with a visa to the States.

The elation and incredulity had not yet eased the pain of the many rejections I had suffered at the hands of those Consular Officers at the Embassy. Anyway, thank God for Uncle Sam! I feel that the piece of land on the West Coast that he signed over to me and the money he sent to help to pad up my bank account really helped me to get through this time.

With nervous excitement, I anxiously await the call to board the aircraft. I glance at my watch for what must be the hundredth time in the last few minutes. I'd better sit back and relax, we won't be boarding for another hour or so. The buzz of chatter from fellow passengers fills the air, some were loudly extolling the virtues of America, others recounting their Embassy sagas, while some, talking to their relatives in New York, were shouting their new arrival time into cell phones. Amidst the din, I observe those around me, trying to imagine who some of my soon-to-be travelling companions were and what they were thinking. The man in the business suit looked impatient. He kept pulling papers out of his attaché case, reading them for a few minutes, all the while checking the time on an expensive-looking wristwatch. I guess he must be some executive wondering if the delayed departure would make him late for his appointment in New York. But is wha' really going on with this one dressed in shorts and winter boots? She looks like a university student. Wasn't that a style from the sixties or seventies? Or is it back in fashion? Sometimes it's hard to keep up. What I know for sure is that she will soon have to ditch those boots when she steps into the summer heat. What about this woman next to me dressed to the ninety-nines in her Sunday-best dress, stockings and fresh hairdo? It looks like she's making her first trip overseas. Every now and again, she dabs at her eyes with a pink, lace-trimmed handkerchief. I had seen her before she checked in. A busload of her relatives had come to see her off. They all seemed to be in a festive mood, eating, listening to music and talking at the top of their voices, until it was time for her to check in. Then they all burst into tears. I wonder how she felt about that! I certainly won't want anybody to be crying like that when I'm about to get on a plane.

The crackling of the intercom interrupts my thoughts. Finally, I hear the announcement we have all been waiting for: "Ladies and gentlemen we are about to commence boarding for our service to JFK, New York. Please have your passports and boarding passes ready." I inch forward in the line, trying to hide the weight of my bag. I really don't want them to take my bag and check it in. I have too much good stuff in it. Bye, bye Guyana, time for new places and different faces! Brown, mud trails snaking through lush greenery greet me as I look down to say goodbye. Whenever I do this, I can't help reflecting on the name they have for us in some of the Caribbean islands - 'mud heads'. No problem, this mud head is on her way to the bright lights of the Big Apple!

The insistent nudging from the elbow of the passenger beside me rouses me. He is pointing excitedly at the tops of buildings and maze of streets that mark our arrival in New York. I follow the trail of passengers to Immigration, rehearsing my responses to the officer in my head.
"I'm here for a short vacation with my relatives, Sir."
"I will be staying six weeks, Sir."
"I will be in New York and Illinois, Sir."
My heart feels like it's thumping it's way out of my chest and up into my throat. I just pray that he doesn't hear it and think I'm too nervous.

"Well hello, Uncle Sam! I'm here! New York, at last! I'm so glad you're here to pick me up! I won't know where to turn and which taxi to take."

As we leave the highway, I am so engrossed in taking in the sights that I miss most of what my uncle is saying to me. Hmm, so *this* is Brooklyn! *This* is New York! Was I expecting too much? I know every city has it's good and bad but I didn't expect to see so much that was familiar, like bags of garbage on the sidewalks and women with ordinary-looking clothes and rollers in their hair on the street! It looks as though some people worse off over here than back home! Brown brick, brown brick, everywhere brown brick... Brown brick rising from the ground and reaching up ten and more storeys into the air... Beneath the dirt and grime, I could see evidence of a glorious past etched into the stone on many of the buildings we pass...

"We're here!" Uncle Sam's announcement interrupted my reflections.

Wow! Everybody is over at Aunty Vilma's house today. It's so good to see them! It seems like some folks were just waiting for me to get there to collect their stuff and then rush off.

"Sorry, cuz. I got to go to work at 4.00. Thanks for the guava cheese and tamarind balls. The children really looking forward..."

"Girl, you know I can't tell the last day I had bora with dried shrimps! I gon' cook dis shrimps tomorrow!"

Of course, you can't have catching up without aggravation. People asking stupid questions about if Georgetown stop flooding or if they still have mosquitoes! I don't want to rock the boat though. I really want to ask them if they don't have flooding and mosquitoes in the States! I'm not going to say anything about the roaches I can see playing hide-and-seek between Aunty Vilma's fridge and stove...

"So, Pauline, when you going back?"
"But, Pauline, why you going back?"
"Pauline, you ain't going back, right?
I have to answer those questions constantly whenever I meet someone from back home. Are people asking me when I'm returning so they can send stuff with me? Why do others feel I won't want to go back? Do they feel that once here, my only option would be to stay? I have to remind them that I have my good job back home!

It would be good to leave the hustle and bustle of New York for a while. The last two weeks have been a whirlwind of activity, of friends and relatives dropping by to visit or taking me out to see the various sights - The Empire State Building, Coney Island, The Statue of Liberty, Times Square ... In some ways Brooklyn and Manhattan seemed like two different worlds. When I was in Brooklyn, it was easy to forget that I was in the States. If I wanted to, I could eat the same kinds of food I'm used to back home. I could even buy water coconut out of a cart from a man on the street corner. Also, I kept bumping into people I know - like Jasper Fredricks. He was a big bank manager back home. Well now he's the security guard at the bank over here! He pretended not to see or hear me when I tried to say hello to him. I guess he must be ashamed. As if I care! He ain't picking nobody pocket! It's honest labour. I'm sure he's earning enough money to support his family. Anyway, enough of that!

I'm happy for the opportunity to see other places in the States. I'm really looking forward to spending some time with my friend Christine who lives in Illinois. She left Guyana right after high school and has only been back a few times. This bus trip is supposed to be twenty-something long hours! Just imagine I can get on a nice, air-conditioned bus and travel for so many hours! I wonder when we're going to be able to do this back home? I would love to see Kaieteur Falls and the Rupununi Savannahs. But I ain't flying in there on them small planes. And the mini-bus and truck trip on the dirt roads would only break up my back and toss up my inside. So I don't know if I would ever get to see those sights!

The man next to me is intent on conversing. I guess he heard me talking on the phone with Christine. "You have an accent. Where are you visiting from?" I have to try to be pleasant. I feel like telling him that he has an accent too... "Oh you know, my daughter is on a mission trip in Liberia right now!" Okay! So he thinks I'm from Africa? I try explaining to him that **Guy-ana** is in South America. So his next question is: "How did you learn English?" So now I have to explain about our history, and I tell him that we are really a Caribbean country. "Oh, I *thought* your accent sounded Jamaican!" My silent scream for help goes unheard. He now proceeds to ask all kinds of questions about my family and me. It's strange that people would ask a total stranger such personal questions! I decided to pretend to sleep just to shut him up.

My legs are stiff, and my feet swollen by the time I arrive at my destination. It is so good to see Christine! She has all kinds of plans for what we are going to do during my first week in Bloomington: shopping, karaoke, bungee jumping... I have to stop her at that one.

"Girl, like you live among with these people till you get like them! Bungee who? Not me, my dear! I plan to go back to Guyana alive and with all my limbs intact!" Christine laughs and calls me a coward for not being adventurous.

Christine's week off goes by quickly. I know she's happy to have company and to talk about old times. I don't understand how she could live out here so far away from all her family and friends. For the second week of my visit, I'm on my own because Christine is back at work. Since she told me I wasn't adventurous, I'm going to try exploring on my own. The streets here are so much quieter than those in New York. I am the only one waiting for the bus and when it arrives, there are only a few passengers on it: - two elderly white women sitting up front near the driver and four black teens down at the back laughing and talking at the top of their voices. At the next stop a Hispanic family gets on. It's funny how the parents are speaking to the children in Spanish, but they respond in English! I strain to catch a few words, but I have difficulty understanding them.

I'm surprised that the mall is so full on a week day. I didn't think that so many adults would be in the mall during times when they should be at work. I don't really want to shop, I just want to window shop and look at the prices of these things to see if they are cheaper here than in New York. As I make my way through the aisles, I feel as though I'm being followed. I turn quickly only to see the sales girl pretend to be straightening the blouse on one of the hangers. Why am I surprised! I experienced the same thing in a few stores in New York. I'm not in the mood for it today, so I leave and go and sit in one of the massaging chairs, put in a dollar and try to relieve my stress. I then head to the supermarket. I want to surprise Christine and cook some cook-up rice for dinner.

Before heading back, I stop at the Customer Service counter to get some change for my bus fare. As I approach the counter, the clerk moves away from the register and starts packing items in a cart. After waiting quietly for a few minutes, I clear my throat and rap my knuckles on the counter. She looks up, looks through me and then continues with what she's doing. I try to contain my indignation as I contemplate my next move. Just then, an octogenarian with sparse flaxen curls shuffles up to the counter. Miss Busy Bee behind the counter flits over and chirps, "Who was here first?" The blood in my veins shoot past boiling point and I know that my face is the shade of a ripe eggplant. How Christine could have survived in a place like this for some many years, I wonder. I knew then that it was time to head back to New York.

Somehow, things are different in New York though. Everybody is busy. So, I'm on my own now! But because I like to be on the go, I will have to learn to get around on my own. I can't sit and wait for anyone to take me around. Another thing that's different is the way Aunty Vilma keeps fussing about her bills. It's funny, she's not speaking directly to me, not telling me not to make calls or to be careful with my use of her appliances, but almost every day she makes a point of commenting about how different life is here than in Guyana. Her constant chorus is how much the utility bills have gone up and how all you living for in this America is to pay bills... I'm going to make sure I buy a phone card when I go out tomorrow. I'm also being very careful about not watching too much T.V during the day.

The thought that I might be overstaying my welcome keeps bugging me. I think I should better start making plans to go back home. The thought nags me constantly but the truth of the matter is that I'm not really ready to go home as yet. I can't go home with my two long hands after six weeks in America! Everybody will be looking forward to a small piece or some kind of 'praggs' when I get back. I can just imagine them coming to the house:
"Eh, eh gyurl wha yuh brin' fuh me!"
"Well, yuh know I come fuh me praggs!"
"So when de barrel coming? Ah hope it gat in some queen size stockings, Coach bags and Calvin Klein jeans!"
Lawd! I don't know is what these people really think it is at all!

Ever since I arrived, Uncle Sam was trying to encourage me to stay. He mentioned different things - a live-in job in Long Island, taking care of old people in Manhattan... I told him I wasn't interested. I came on a holiday, not to do domestic and care-giving work! Furthermore, I had no plans to stay in this place. Well he said I should think about it. I don't know... I guess it's the only thing I could do on the side and make a little small piece quietly seeing that I'm only here on a holiday visa. But I could just imagine what people back home would say if they hear that I'm doing domestic work here in America! They would think I'm stooping low But that's not their business.

Why should I care? It's honest labour! People will always talk and criticize. I could at least pack a barrel or two and send home. Nobody in Guyana ain't got to know is what kind of job I was doing in America. They're only going to be interested in what I have to give them! Look how hard I had to fight to get a visa to come over here in the first place! I better make the most of it! I don't know if I will get a chance to come back! But suppose I run into trouble with Immigration? That would be a big embarrassment! Imagine my face in the newspapers as a deportee! I wonder if I should take the chance. I was planning to spend six weeks but when I got here, the Immigration Officer gave me six months to stay... Look, you never know with this place... I reach for the phone.

"Hello? Uncle Sam...

THE CHAIR BY THE WINDOW

The chirping of bird-song wafts through the window on early morning breezes. As the first rays of sunlight force their way between the curtains their warm strokes caress her face and tug at the covers. *I have to get up now! I must have over-slept,* Gloria thinks, as she turns over in the bed to check on her husband. The crisp, smooth sheet and plump pillow that greet her are reminders of the harsh reality she now has to live with. After fifty-five years of marriage, she is all alone. Trembling, she crawls back between the sheets. There is no need to wake Phillip. No need to take him to the bathroom. No need to help him to the chair by the window that looked out on to their street.

She eventually responds to the hollow in her stomach and pulls herself out of bed. The soothing warmth of hot chocolate trickles down, caressing the aching cavities and stroking away the pain in her stomach. She looks up just in time to see her next-door neighbour heading out to work. "Bye, bye, chile," she waves and calls out. Just then, she looks on in wonderment as a youth from a few houses down the street races by on his new mountain bike, smartly clad in his school uniform. *Eh, eh! Neighbour James son so big now that he riding to school by himself!* She urges him to be careful as he wobbles in his attempt to steer the bike with one hand and wave to her with the other. She was now experiencing what Phillip had, for so much time in that chair near the window.

From this vantage point, there was a clear view of the street and all the neighbourhood goings on.

That old, wooden rocking chair had a lot of history. It had been her mother's favourite seat after she had come to live with them when she lost her husband. It had really been his chair and she just couldn't bear to part with it. Her silken white curls had graced that corner for some twenty years before she retired to bed for the final time at age ninety-eight. Gloria remembers her mother greeting the neighbours and calling out bits of advice to the schoolchildren from that seat: "Careful, Sonny! Walk in the corner!"
"Hello Miss! Pick up that sweetie paper!"
"Morning, Jamesie. You look dapper today!"
Sitting in that corner, she even did her share of household chores – she picked rice and callaloo, shelled peas, grated coconut, cut up greens - all from her favourite seat near the window.

About two weeks after Ma passed away; Gloria rearranged the living room and moved the rocker to the other end of the room. She could not bear to see it sitting by the window, empty…

She racked her brain for a few minutes trying to remember how the chair had got back to its previous position. She then recalled the night two cars had collided right in front of the house. Philip had put it there so he could sit and take in all the action. It remained there ever since, and it soon became his favourite seat.

Philip had always been a very active person. He went out to work until he was in his seventies. He was a very good teacher and loved his daily interactions with the youths. He wasn't ready to give up teaching, but the new Principal had said that the older folks should give the young teachers a chance. So, they asked him to consider retirement. It was with great reluctance that he left his beloved profession. What could he do? He spent his days reading and observing the flow of life from the chair by the window.

At eighty-two, Gloria was still actively taking care of her chores both inside and outside of the house. She could only sit with Philip at meal times and in the evening when they enjoyed their nightly game of checkers. He would then continue to fill her in with the things he had seen and the people with whom he had interacted from his vantage point beside the window.

The hollow in her stomach is still there, but the cup of hot chocolate has perked her up a little. *I guess it would take a long time for the empty feeling to go away,* she thinks, as she contemplates the parched earth in her garden down below, realising that it is calling out for water to quench its thirst. The rose bush begs to be groomed and the zinnias and gerberas cry out for help from the invasive weeds. She draws her head back inside, leans back and tries to decide whether she should try to begin to tackle the garden later or just pay someone to get it done...

"Morning Ms. Gloria. How you keeping?"
"Morning chile," she laughs as she realises that Clarise is late for work again! Philip used to laugh every morning as she rushed through the gate. She would look up and call out her greeting to him. It soon begins to dawn on her that she has missed many of the activities in the neighbourhood. Elaine's daughter walks by with an added stiffness in her gait as she pushes a stroller. *When did that happen?* **Ring! Ring!** The insistent ring of the phone urges her up. Her grandson, Jimmy, is calling to check on her. He invites her to go to spend some time with him in Parika. She agrees with him that it would be a good idea, but she puts him off. "Give me a few weeks. I have to sort out some things at this end,"

Midday arrives before she knows it, and she is dismayed that she really hasn't done anything all morning long. She hasn't showered, nor has she cooked. She decides to take it easy, heat up the left-over soup, and spend the rest of the day relaxing near the window.

Knock! Knock! Knock ... That knocking has been going on for some time... She wonders if her neighbour was doing repairs on his house. She could hear the sound of hammering in the distance. **Knock! Knock! Knock**... "Aunty!

Aunty, you home? Inside!" **Knock knock knock!** *Eh, eh! Wait! Someone is knocking at my door!*

"Come in, chile. I must have dozed off," she explains, on opening the door for her great-niece, Theresa. The bowl of half-eaten soup is still sitting on the ledge below the windowsill. Before leaving, Theresa promises to return the next day to spend some time with her.

Lying in bed that night, Gloria tries to decide whether or not to accept Jimmy's invitation to go to Parika. *I really don't want to be a burden on anyone. A change of scene would be nice for a week or two, though. But whom could I get to stay in this house? I can't leave it empty, not with how things are in the city these days! Maybe I could ask Theresa...*

She is up at the crack of dawn and heads to the kitchen to prepare breakfast for herself and Theresa. Theresa is there bright and early the next morning as promised. The first thing she does is to put on the radio. Oh how Gloria revels in the 'Golden Oldies' on 98.1 FM! She had forgotten that it was the norm to have those on Thursday mornings. The sounds of Elvis Presley, Dionne Warwick, Sam Cooke, Otis Redding, Patsy Cline and The Temptations accompany them as they clean windows, change curtains, scrub floors, rearrange furniture, throw away and burn, to their hearts' content.

She is happy to have some company. As night falls, it is now time for them to relax. "Come, chile," she calls out to Theresa, "let's sit and rest now. Bring your chair over here by the window and let's drink some Milo and play a game of checkers."

She heads over to the chair by the window only to realise it's not there! "Theresa! Where is my chair?" *These young people like to do things their way. Where has she put my chair?* She wonders as she attempts to locate the chair. The rocker is not in any of the rooms. A search of the storeroom downstairs proves fruitless. Theresa's sly smile greets her as she drags her tired body up the stairs. "Have you given up looking now, Aunty? That chair is not for you. Let's sit over here and plan tomorrow's work and then you can beat me at a game or two of checkers." Reluctantly, Gloria follows her niece to the other end of the room and plops herself down on the sofa. *Tomorrow I'm going to check the storage shed in the yard to see if that is where she put my chair...*

As they discuss the next day's chores, Gloria realises that she has so much to keep her busy; she really has no time to be idle. *Maybe Theresa does have a point. How could I sit in the chair by the window when I still have so much work to do?*

Before heading to bed, she checks to make sure the keys to the storage shed are still hanging on the hook in the kitchen.

THE WASHERWOMAN'S TALE

Scrruuuks! Scrrruuks! Scrruuks! Her worn, wrinkled, suds-covered hands kneaded the garments on the scrubbing board. From time to time, she lifted the end of her wet apron to mop the sweat that poured down her face. This is her last load for the day. Soon she will wend her way home to her family, stopping at the market to buy something for the next day's meal…

"Ms. Claribel, my Mommy send this for you."
"T'ank you, chile. Tell your Mommy I say t'anks". She took the envelope with her wages from little Maisy and stuffed it in her bosom before turning to complete her task.

"Ms. Claribel, why your hands not smooth and nice like my Mommy's hands?"
"Ms. Claribel, why you always wearing those old shoes?
"Ms. Claribel, why you have your head tied up like that? I never see your hair."
"Lil chile, why you asking so many questions, eh? Run along and play with your brothers and sisters an' leave me to do my work!"
"Ms. Claribel, I don't really want to play with my brothers and sisters. I have a new book. You could read it for me when you finish washing?
"Tell you what, Maisy, I will read it for you today if *you* promise to read it for me when I come back next week."

Ten minutes later she settled little Maisy on her lap and read her the story. It was a wonderful tale about a young girl who had had a hard life and how she met and married a handsome prince.

"Thanks Ms. Claribel! It's a really nice story! Who teach you to read so good?"
"I went to school you know?" she replied as she closed the gate and headed home.

As Claribel Dennis wended her way home, she was oblivious to the blistering mid-afternoon sun that dried her dress to a crisp…

<<Yes, I went to school. I had wanted to become a schoolteacher. Now look at me! Thirty years old with seven children turnin' meh hair grayer by the day. But God is good! Geoffrey is almost sixteen and he just get a hold-on with Mr. Sawyers in town. So at least he gon' learn a trade and soon he gon' be able to help heself. The other younger ones, they tryin' with their schoolin'. Thank God for that! One day soon I ain't gon' have to slave over other people washin'. >>

<<Who would understand my situation? Certainly not little Maisy! She was too young to understand the nervous excitement I felt as I climbed into the car. Look at me, sitting in the front seat of Mr. Xavier's brand new Morris Oxford motorcar! It was a special treat. Brother Joe was taking me

home in the plantation manager's car! I remember wishing my school friends could see me. I was imaginin' how envious they would all be.>> Time had done nothing to dull the memories of that day...
"So Clari, I see you growing into quite a big young lady",
"Oh! Uh... thanks Brother Joe. I gon' soon turn fourteen."
"That's a nice dress you wearing. Your Mommy sew it?"

<<Even now almost sixteen years later, the flush of warmth still rushes to my face as I think of how he had said those words. And it was not just the words; Brother Joe was looking at me in a strange way. I was anxious for the car ride to be over. I longed to get home. Lord knows if I had the sense then that I have now, nothing like Joseph Layne would have gotten the better of me! That is why even though I ain't finish my schoolin', I makin' sure my children get a good education and I teach them to have road sense too! I don't talk in parables like my mother used to do to me and my sisters. It was always some nonsense like "If you mek yuhself grass, cow gon' eat yuh!" Or, "If yuh don' go to crab dance yuh can't get mud!"Now, how in heaven's name we was supposed to understand that she was really tryin' to tell us to be good, virtuous girls? Well, I guess we did understand in a way...but they just didn't come straight out and tell us about the facts of life. Me, I don't mince matters. I tell my girls like it is. They have to understand that it's not just the young boys they have to beware of, and it's not just strangers. Sometimes is the same people who you know does turn 'round and tek advantage o' yuh.>>

As she opened the gate to enter her yard, Claribel looked around to make sure everything was in order. The yard was clean; the chickens had been fed and put in their coop. Good! That meant the children were inside doing their homework.

For the next few hours she busied herself taking care of her family's needs. The younger children needed help with their homework. She cooked and served dinner and made sure everyone was in bed before she took a seat in her favourite chair in the verandah. As she sat looking out on the still, pitch-black night, little Maisy and her questions came to mind once more.

<<Maisy, my child, if only you knew... I was once a young girl like you. Maybe not as well-to-do, but full of life, joy, hopes and aspirations too. I went to school and learned my lessons well. Never for once thought my life could become a living hell. I was going to be a teacher, you know... The children, I loved, so I'd help them to grow, learn and excel... and, they'd love me as well...>> "Here I go, again... maybe I should have been a poet!" she laughed softly.

<<That was one of my dreams, Maisy, child: to teach, to write, to make my parents proud. I used to go down to the big town to help my older sister with her little ones. There is where my troubles began... And he was not a stranger. He was someone I know quite well. You see dear Maisy, Mr. Joe was like an uncle to me. He was married to my sister's

husband's sister. Is that too complicated for you? Well, let me break it down a bit. My sister, Yvonne, was married to Brother Larry. He is my brother-in-law. Well Mr. Joe's wife and Brother Larry are brother and sister. So, you see, he was like family and he was always over by my sister's house, gaffing and drinking with Brother Larry. So sometimes he would offer to take me home in his car. Actually, it was not really *his* car. He was the chauffeur for the estate manager Mr. Xavier. For a country-girl like me that was a real treat to be sitting in that shiny, new Morris Oxford driving up the Corentyne coast.

Learn from me Maisy. Learn from me. Never trust a man! He start sweet-talkin' me 'bout how pretty I look and how nice I dress and how big I gettin' and before I know it – I was really gettin' big! I mean I had two growin' breasts and a swellin' belly that I was tryin' to hide from my mother! Lord! I was so frightened I didn't know what to do! My dear child, I don't expect you to understand everything now. One day you will understand how my life turn up-side-down! What shame and embarrassment my whole family went through! My poor mother, God bless the dead, nearly go out she head when she realise what was happenin' to me and *who* was responsible!

What a scandal! A young girl like me, still in school, no husband and a big belly… My parents ain't had nowhere to send me to hide. So, we had to endure all the shame right here in the village. Learn from me my child: a man does no wrong! It's always we women-folk that does get the blame.

You would not believe the things people in this village and beyond say 'bout me.

- It serve she right! Who tell she fuh tek drop in cyar by she-self!
- Dat is what does happen when lil gal like throw dey-self in front o' big man! They does get wha' they lookin' for!
- Well, Ms. Big Shot meet she metre! She always walkin' 'round this village wid she head in a book. Now she ga' fuh hang it in shame!

At first, I didn't want to tell Ma who was responsible, but she put some good licks in me, and I had to talk. I know you can't imagine me trials, chile. In the good year of our Lord 1925 when I just turn 15, I find meself with a chile to raise! I couldn't go back to school. The only work I could do in my village was cleanin', cookin' and washin' for other people.>>

"Clara, what you doing out there on the verandah by yuhself so late?" Yuh ain't comin' to bed?" Jonathan's voice brought her back to the present. Her husband was early to bed as usual. After a few minutes, she got up, went in, shut the door, blew out the kerosene lamps and eased her aching body into the bed where her husband was already snoring lightly. She reached across and caressed his large, calloused hands as she settled in for the night.

Jonathan had moved into the village to work on the estate just around Geoffrey's fifth birthday. He would be playing cards and drinking with the other young village lads in Mr. Sam's rum-shop on Friday afternoons. Claribel dreaded passing the rum-shop but that was the only route to her home. She no longer heard the insults and taunts the young men hurled in her direction, just the rumbling chorus and the shrill, mocking laughter that came after each rumble. One day, however, the sharp rebuke that brought the taunts to a premature halt caused her to glance across at the shop. Someone she had never seen before was admonishing his companions. He then left the group and as he accompanied her home, he apologised for his friends' bad behavior and introduced himself. Within six months, she was Mrs. Jonathan Dennis.

Claribel brushed her husband's hands with her lips and snuggled against the curve of his body.
<<So here I am, an honourable, married woman. Marriage helped to remove some of the shame and stigma. As for Jonathan, I know he ain't no angel, he loves the bottle and sometimes his temper does get the better of him, but he's a good man at heart. His labourer wages barely enough; so I still got to do washin' and ironin' for people. I so glad Geoffrey learnin' the lil trade. Soon he gon' be able to support heself and he might able to give me a lil small piece so I don't have to work so hard...>>

Thoughts and memories filled Claribel's head and sleep eluded her that night. She knew what she had to do. There was not a moment to spare. She got up, taking care not to disturb her husband's sleep, went into the kitchen and removed the worn school notebook she kept on a shelf in the broom cupboard. The second half of this book that she once used as a diary, was now used to write shopping lists, keep track of the household spending and such things. She flipped through the pages and read her first diary entry, dated Saturday April 26, 1924. She took the pencil, crossed out some things and inserted others. When Claribel realised there were no clean pages left in the old notebook she went over to the corner where the children kept their schoolbags. She searched frantically until she found those books they had hardly used, ripped a few pages from each one and sat down again at the kitchen table. Even though the flicker of the flame from the lamp and the smoke that emanated from the worn wick slowed her down somewhat, she kept going, stopping every now and again to rub her aching eyes.

Claribel jumped out of a deep slumber when she felt Jonathan shaking her. An old school book and pages filled with scribbles surrounded her. He called out to her, "Woman! You mean to tell me you didn't sleep in de bed las' night! Is wha' you spen' de whole night say you writin'?" Claribel's tired, swollen eyes held a glint of triumph as she squinted up at him and said, "I *had* to do it Jonathan. *I* had to do it. Who else could tell *my* story?"

GLOSSARY

Bad-fashion - greed, envious, bad-behaved.

Bottom-house - the area below houses that are built on stilts.

Box hand (aka 'sou sou' in some countries) - a traditional way of community savings in Caribbean societies where a group of people pool a pre-agreed amount each week or month. A different individual in the group receives the entire amount pooled each week or month until everyone has been paid.

Bush cook - cooking out in the yard (generally in the garden). This is an activity that children and teenagers enjoyed doing, with or without their parents' approval.

Can-can - flouncy, petticoat made of crinoline

Force-ripe - used to describe young girls who pretend they are older than their actual age, or who engage in adult behaviour.

Pot salt - a meddler, always in the thick of things.

Praags - gifts from someone who lives overseas (in a developed country.)

Salt biscuits - crackers.

Sin bearing blossom - something that has come about before its time, because of a transgression (for instance. a teenage pregnancy.)

Small piece – a little bit of cash

Sweet biscuits - cookies.

Talk-name - gossip.

When yuh gat yuh dutty calico doan hang it outside - A Guyanese Creolese proverb. Meaning: Don't expose your own scandalous stories to the public.

Since the language used throughout *Ma Mae's Legacy* is a combination of standard Guyanese English and Guyanese Creolese, the spelling of certain English words is consistent with the way they are written in Guyana and the English-speaking Caribbean.

.

Acknowledgements

I conceived the first few stories of this collection in Guyana in the early 2000s. Over the years, as I worked and re-worked these stories and added to their number, friends, family-members and colleagues took the time to read and provide valuable feedback. Some also helped with editing.

It is with profound gratitude that I thank all of you, who proved to be the village that brought this child into existence. I choose not to list names. You know yourselves and I am eternally grateful for your help.

About The Author

Melva Archer-Persico is a Guyanese-born academic who currently resides in the United Sates. The written word has always fascinated her. Her love of language and literature led her to pursue language teaching as her profession. She teaches Spanish at Clemson University in South Carolina and conducts research in the fields of Hispanic and Caribbean literature and culture. She is married and the mother of two daughters. She is also the author of a collection of poems entitled *Ink on Paper* (available on Amazon.com).

www.ingramcontent.com/pod-product-compliance
Lightning Source LLC
Chambersburg PA
CBHW050737230626
47052CB00003BA/514